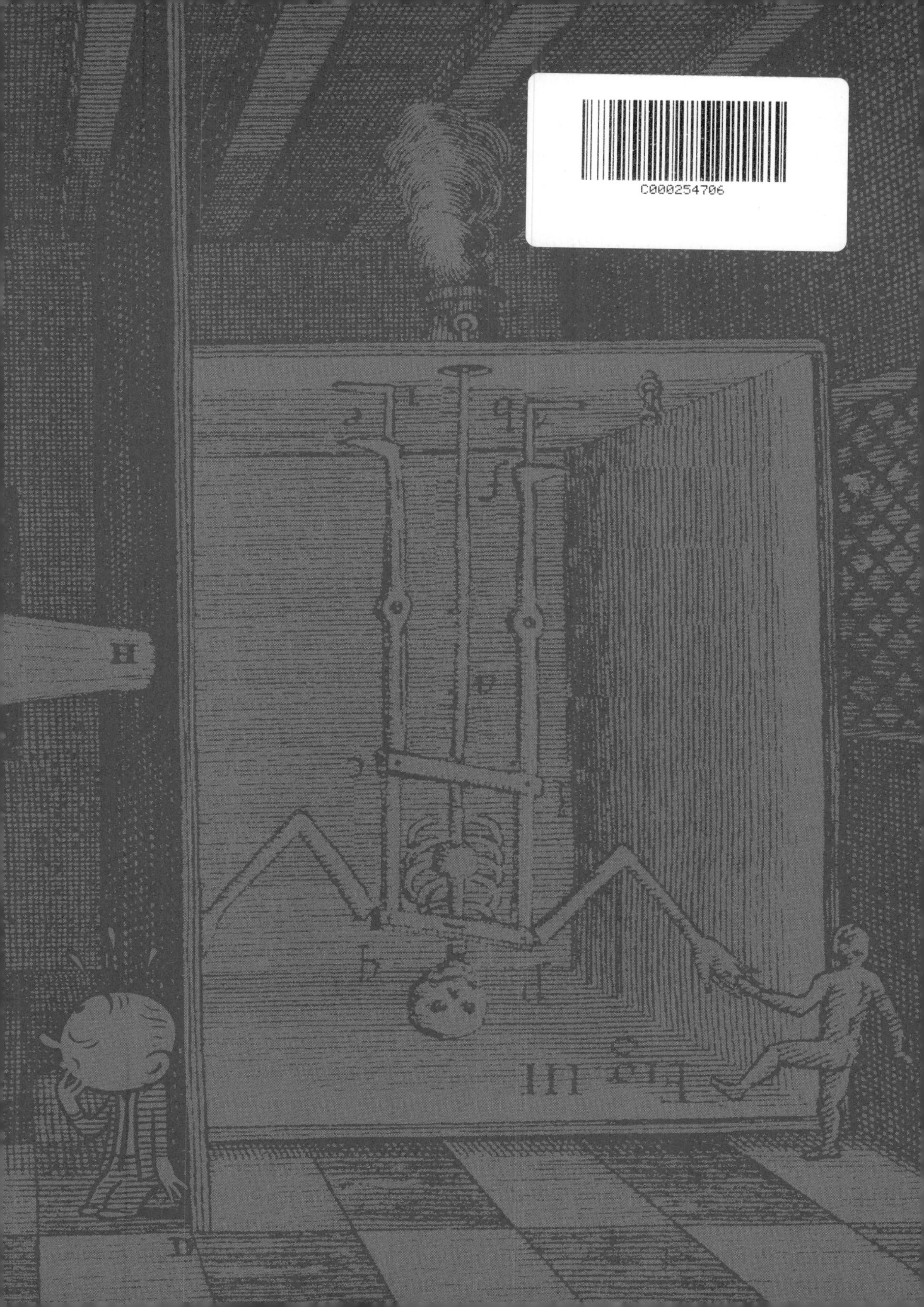

Bardín the Superrealist

His deeds, his utterances, his exploits and his perambulations

Max

FANTAGRAPHICS BOOKS

For Charles Bellver and for Julie Doucet

FANTAGRAPHICS BOOKS, 7563 Lake City Way NE, Seattle WA 98115
Translated by Kim Thompson • Book design by Max
Lettering by Paul Baresh • Promotion by Eric Reynolds
Published by Gary Groth and Kim Thompson
All artwork and text © 2006 Max represented by Ediciones La Cúpula, Spain.
All rights reserved. Permission to quote or reproduce material for reviews or
notices must be obtained from Max or Fantagraphics Books Inc.
Distributed in the U.S. by W.W. Norton and Company, Inc. (212-354-5500)
Distributed in Canada by Raincoast Books (800-663-5714)
Distributed in the United Kingdom by Turnaround Distribution (208-829-3009)

ISBN-10: 1-56097-759-0 • ISBN-13: 978-1-56097-759-9

First printing: May, 2006 • Printed in Spain

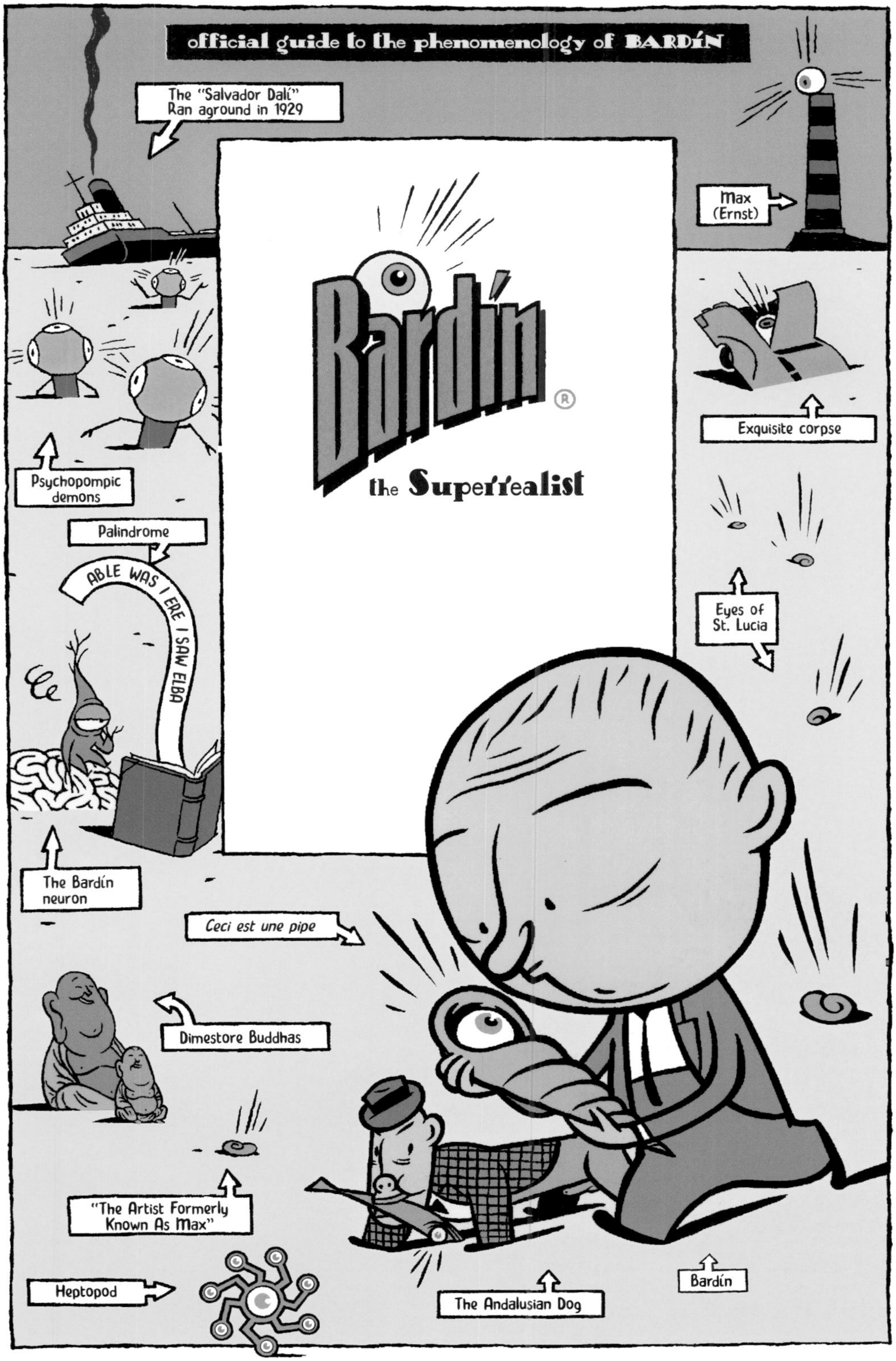
official guide to the phenomenology of BARDÍN
The "Salvador Dalí" Ran aground in 1929
Max (Ernst)
Bardín®
the Superrealist
Psychopompic demons
Exquisite corpse
Palindrome
ABLE WAS I ERE I SAW ELBA
Eyes of St. Lucia
The Bardín neuron
Ceci est une pipe
Dimestore Buddhas
"The Artist Formerly Known As Max"
Heptopod
The Andalusian Dog
Bardín

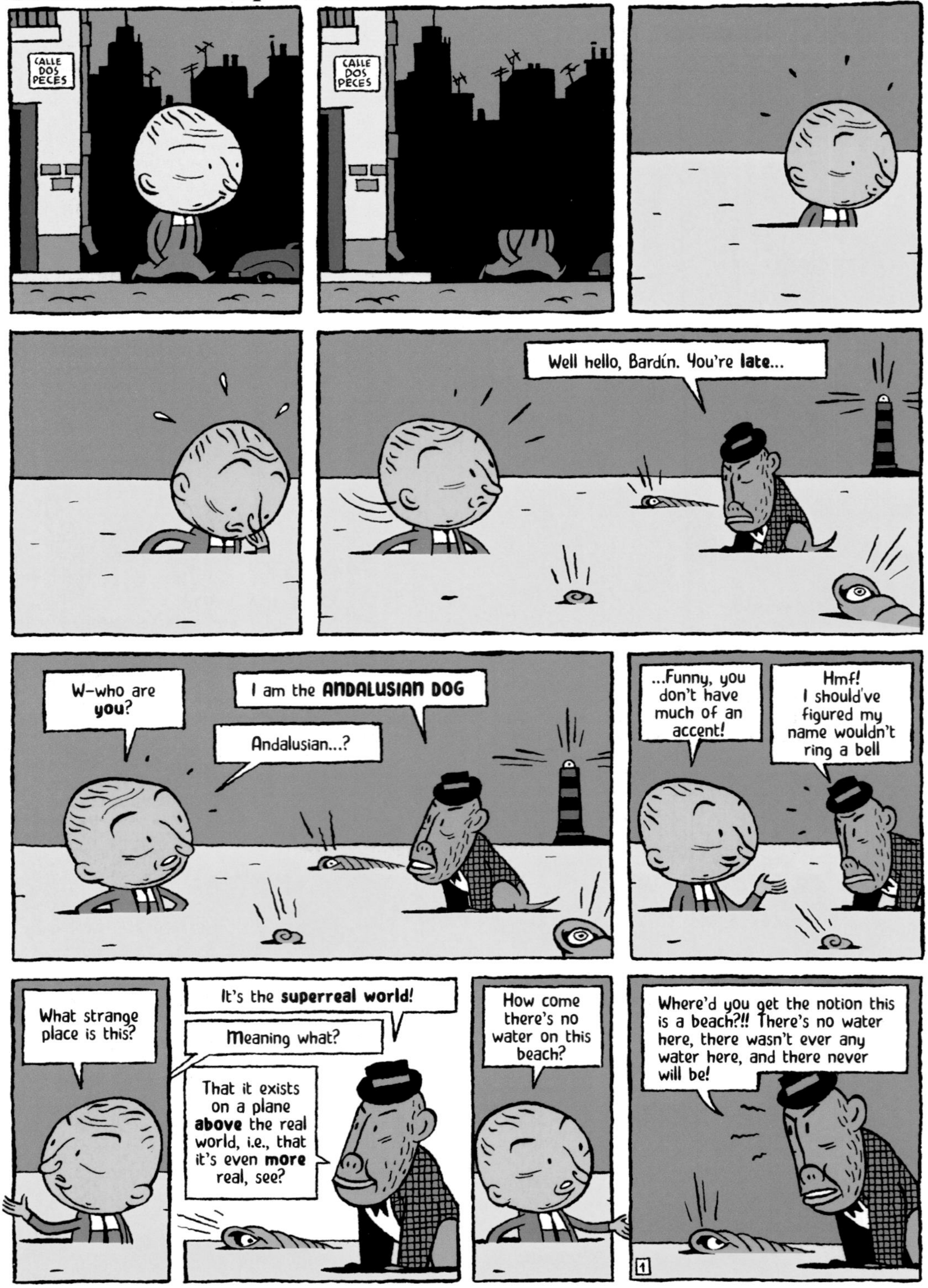
CALLE DOS PECES
CALLE DOS PECES
Well hello, Bardín. You're **late**...
W-who are **you**?
I am the **ANDALUSIAN DOG**
Andalusian...?
...Funny, you don't have much of an accent!
Hmf! I should've figured my name wouldn't ring a bell
What strange place is this?
It's the **superreal world**!
Meaning what?
That it exists on a plane **above** the real world, i.e., that it's even **more** real, see?
How come there's no water on this beach?
Where'd you get the notion this is a beach?!! There's no water here, there wasn't ever any water here, and there never will be!
1

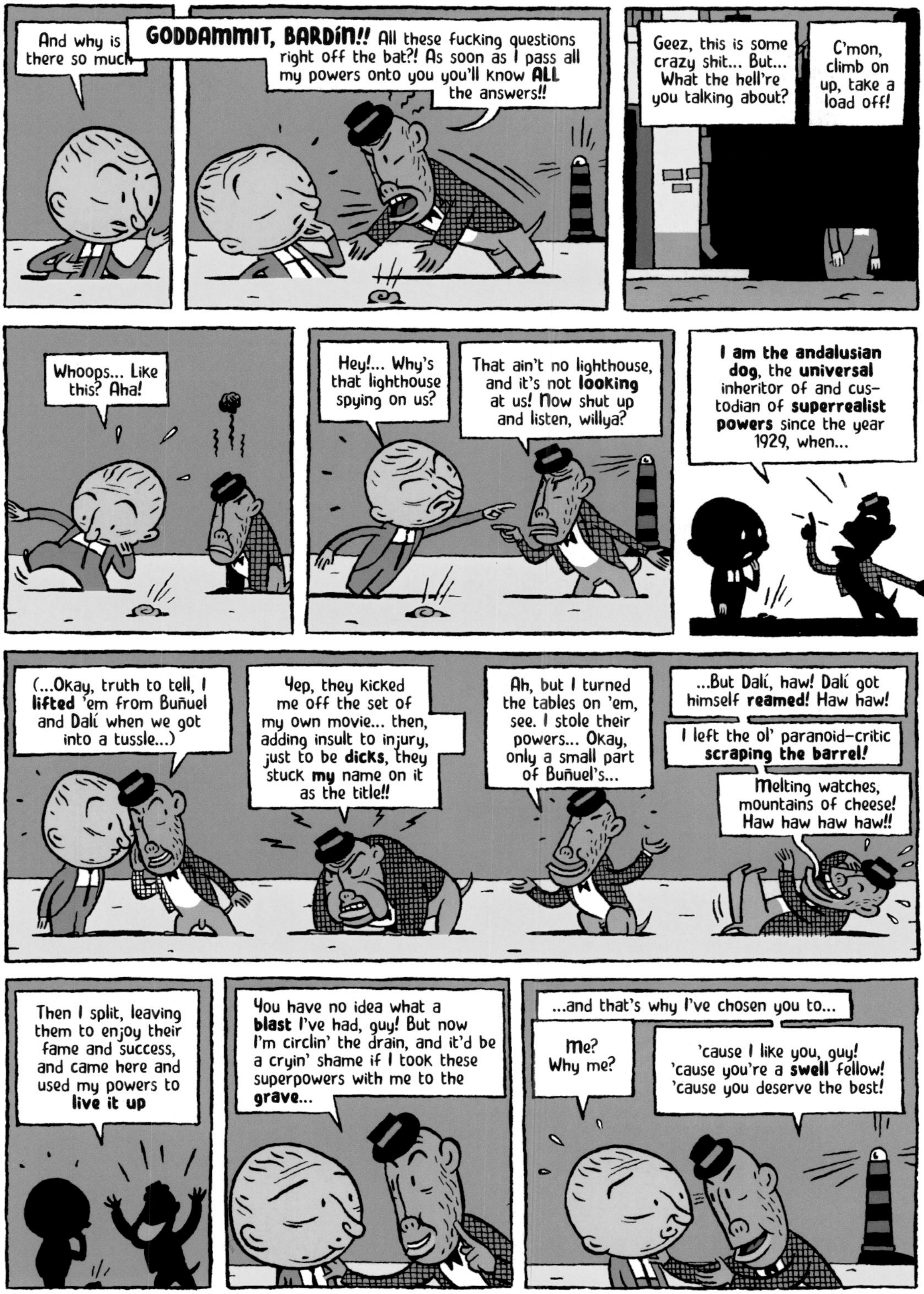

And why is there so much
GODDAMMIT, BARDÍN!! All these fucking questions right off the bat?! As soon as I pass all my powers onto you you'll know ALL the answers!!
Geez, this is some crazy shit... But... What the hell're you talking about?
C'mon, climb on up, take a load off!
Whoops... Like this? Aha!
Hey!... Why's that lighthouse spying on us?
That ain't no lighthouse, and it's not looking at us! Now shut up and listen, willya?
I am the andalusian dog, the universal inheritor of and custodian of superrealist powers since the year 1929, when...
(...Okay, truth to tell, I lifted 'em from Buñuel and Dalí when we got into a tussle...)
Yep, they kicked me off the set of my own movie... then, adding insult to injury, just to be dicks, they stuck my name on it as the title!!
Ah, but I turned the tables on 'em, see. I stole their powers... Okay, only a small part of Buñuel's...
...But Dalí, haw! Dalí got himself reamed! Haw haw!
I left the ol' paranoid-critic scraping the barrel!
Melting watches, mountains of cheese! Haw haw haw haw!!
Then I split, leaving them to enjoy their fame and success, and came here and used my powers to live it up
You have no idea what a blast I've had, guy! But now I'm circlin' the drain, and it'd be a cryin' shame if I took these superpowers with me to the grave...
...and that's why I've chosen you to...
Me? Why me?
'cause I like you, guy! 'cause you're a swell fellow! 'cause you deserve the best!

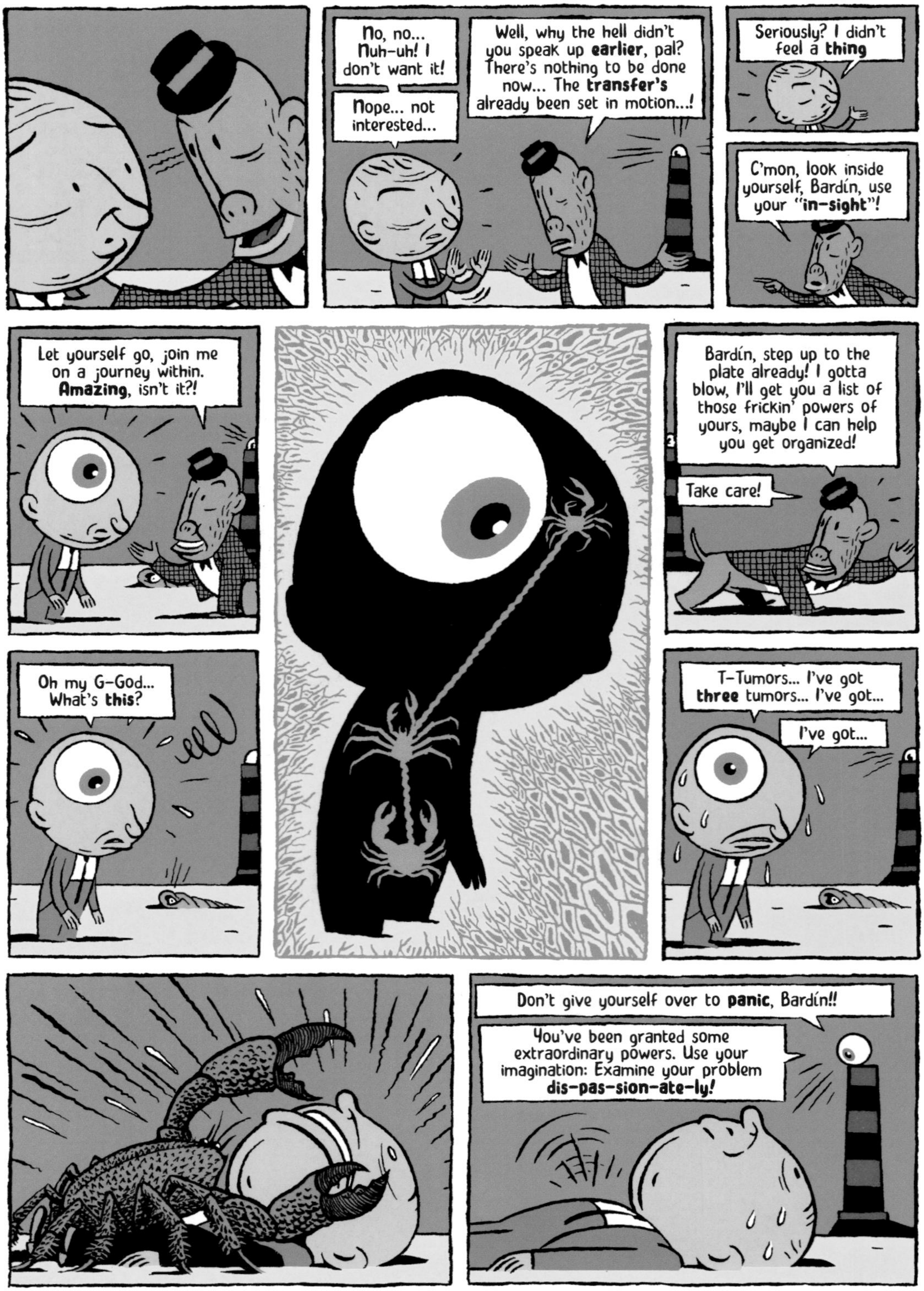
No, no... Nuh-uh! I don't want it!
Nope... not interested...
Well, why the hell didn't you speak up earlier, pal? There's nothing to be done now... The transfer's already been set in motion...!
Seriously? I didn't feel a thing
C'mon, look inside yourself, Bardín, use your "in-sight"!
Let yourself go, join me on a journey within. Amazing, isn't it?!
Bardín, step up to the plate already! I gotta blow, I'll get you a list of those frickin' powers of yours, maybe I can help you get organized!
Take care!
Oh my G-God... What's this?
T-Tumors... I've got three tumors... I've got...
I've got...
Don't give yourself over to panic, Bardín!!
You've been granted some extraordinary powers. Use your imagination: Examine your problem dis-pas-sion-ate-ly!

You're right

Thanks to my **interior vision** I can read my entrails like an open book

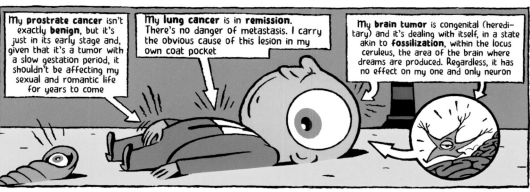

My **prostrate cancer** isn't exactly **benign**, but it's just in its early stage and, given that it's a tumor with a slow gestation period, it shouldn't be affecting my sexual and romantic life for years to come

My **lung cancer** is in **remission**. There's no danger of metastasis. I carry the obvious cause of this lesion in my own coat pocket

My **brain tumor** is congenital (hereditary) and it's dealing with itself, in a state akin to **fossilization**, within the locus ceruleus, the area of the brain where dreams are produced. Regardless, it has no effect on my one and only neuron

Whew! Just a little scare!

All that calls for a **smoke!**

Then again, maybe I oughta quit, ya never know...

Hmm... wonder **how** I started smoking. There's so much that I don't...

Yes, if you remember!

YES! YES, I REMEMBER! OH, GOD... OH, GOD... YES!

You have the power to remember **all** that you've **forgotten!**

BARDÍN remembers

Oh my God... It's... It's... **incredible!**

11

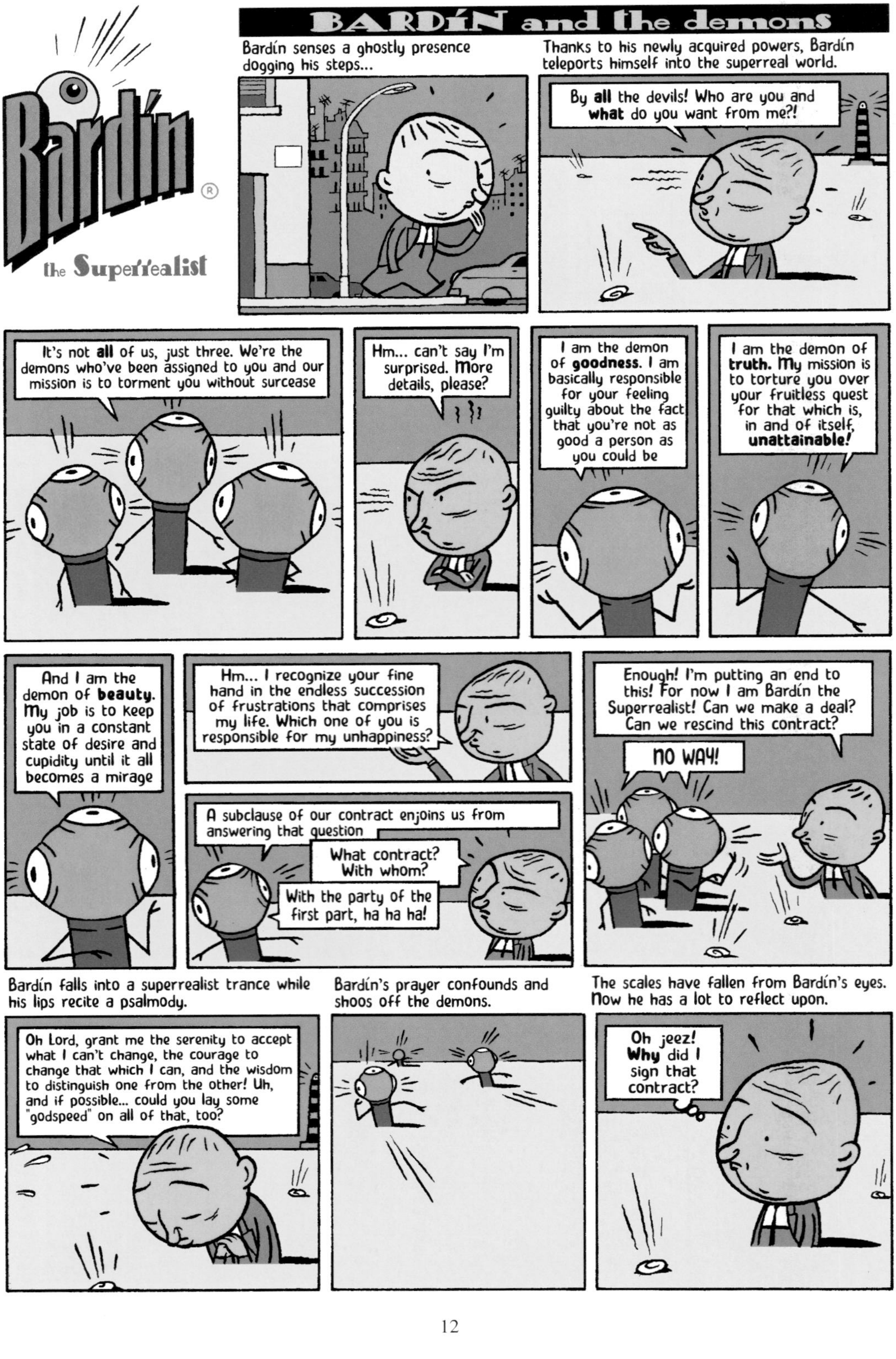
Bardín the Superrealist
BARDÍN and the demons
Bardín senses a ghostly presence dogging his steps...
Thanks to his newly acquired powers, Bardín teleports himself into the superreal world.
By all the devils! Who are you and what do you want from me?!
It's not all of us, just three. We're the demons who've been assigned to you and our mission is to torment you without surcease
Hm... can't say I'm surprised. More details, please?
I am the demon of goodness. I am basically responsible for your feeling guilty about the fact that you're not as good a person as you could be
I am the demon of truth. My mission is to torture you over your fruitless quest for that which is, in and of itself, unattainable!
And I am the demon of beauty. My job is to keep you in a constant state of desire and cupidity until it all becomes a mirage
Hm... I recognize your fine hand in the endless succession of frustrations that comprises my life. Which one of you is responsible for my unhappiness?
A subclause of our contract enjoins us from answering that question
What contract? With whom?
With the party of the first part, ha ha ha!
Enough! I'm putting an end to this! For now I am Bardín the Superrealist! Can we make a deal? Can we rescind this contract?
NO WAY!
Bardín falls into a superrealist trance while his lips recite a psalmody.
Oh Lord, grant me the serenity to accept what I can't change, the courage to change that which I can, and the wisdom to distinguish one from the other! Uh, and if possible... could you lay some "godspeed" on all of that, too?
Bardín's prayer confounds and shoos off the demons.
The scales have fallen from Bardín's eyes. Now he has a lot to reflect upon.
Oh jeez! Why did I sign that contract?

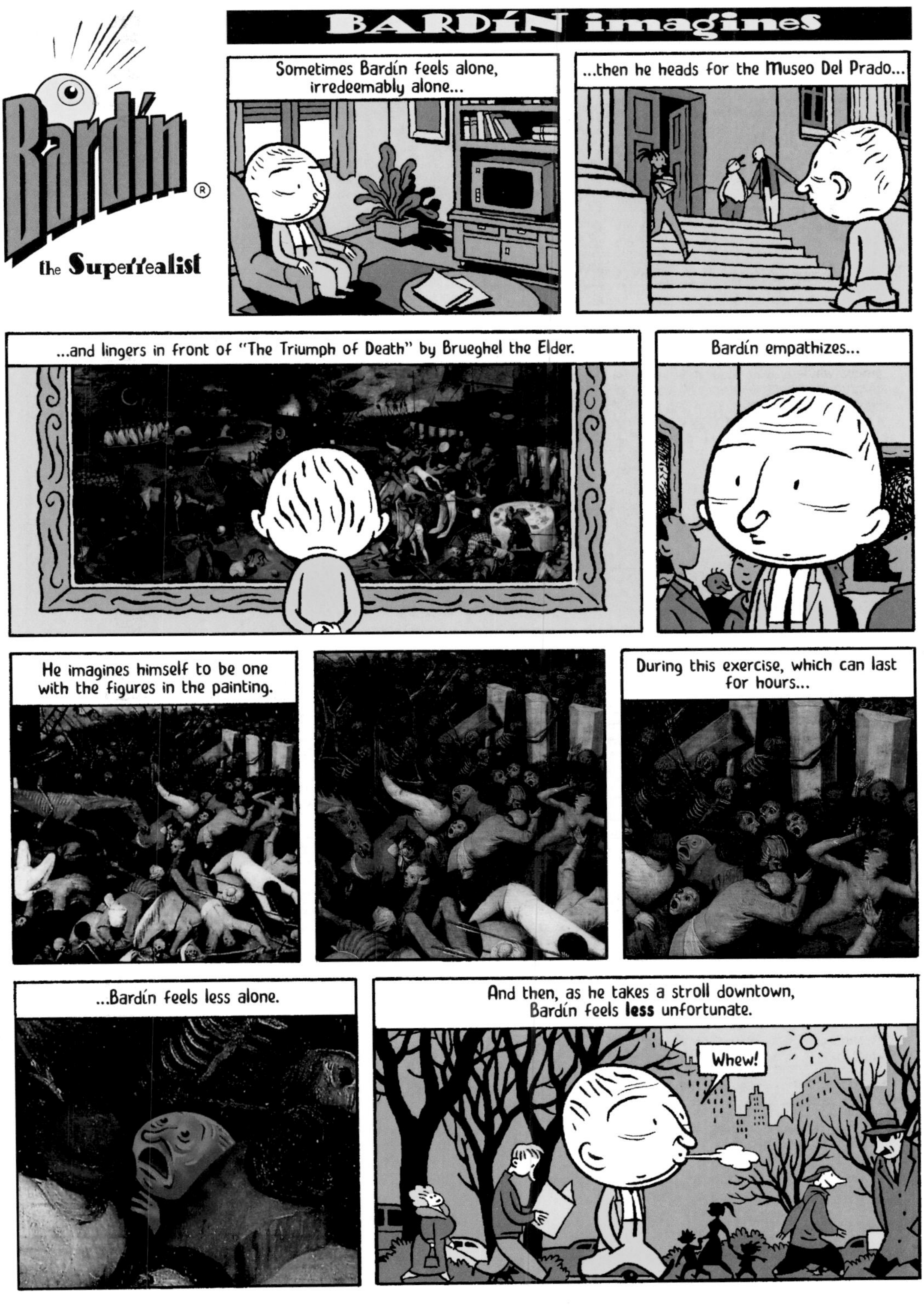
Bardín
the Superrealist
BARDÍN imagines
Sometimes Bardín feels alone, irredeemably alone...
...then he heads for the Museo Del Prado...
...and lingers in front of "The Triumph of Death" by Brueghel the Elder.
Bardín empathizes...
He imagines himself to be one with the figures in the painting.
During this exercise, which can last for hours...
...Bardín feels less alone.
And then, as he takes a stroll downtown, Bardín feels **less** unfortunate.
Whew!

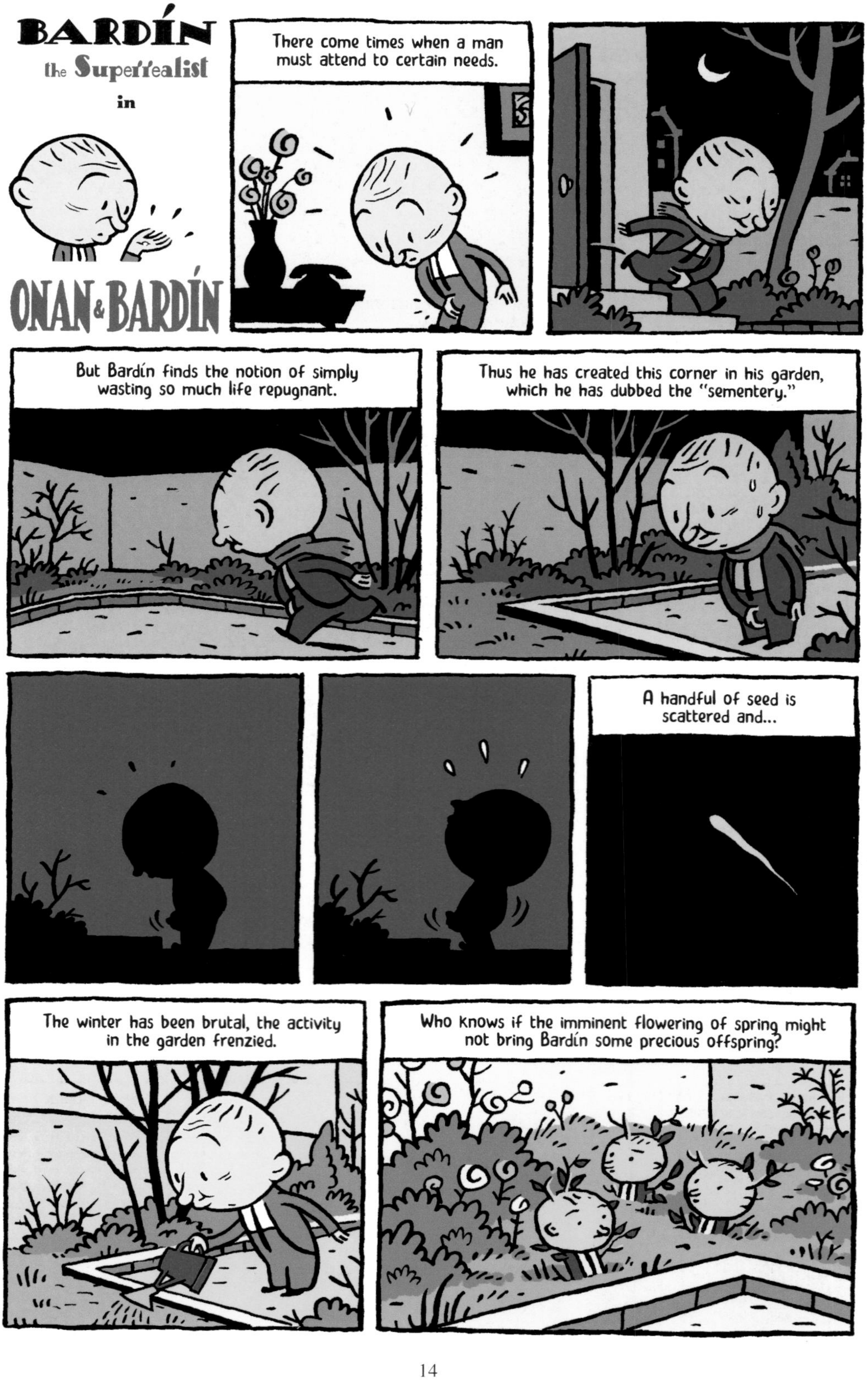
BARDÍN
the Superrealist
in
ONAN & BARDÍN
There come times when a man must attend to certain needs.
But Bardín finds the notion of simply wasting so much life repugnant.
Thus he has created this corner in his garden, which he has dubbed the "sementery."
A handful of seed is scattered and...
The winter has been brutal, the activity in the garden frenzied.
Who knows if the imminent flowering of spring might not bring Bardín some precious offspring?

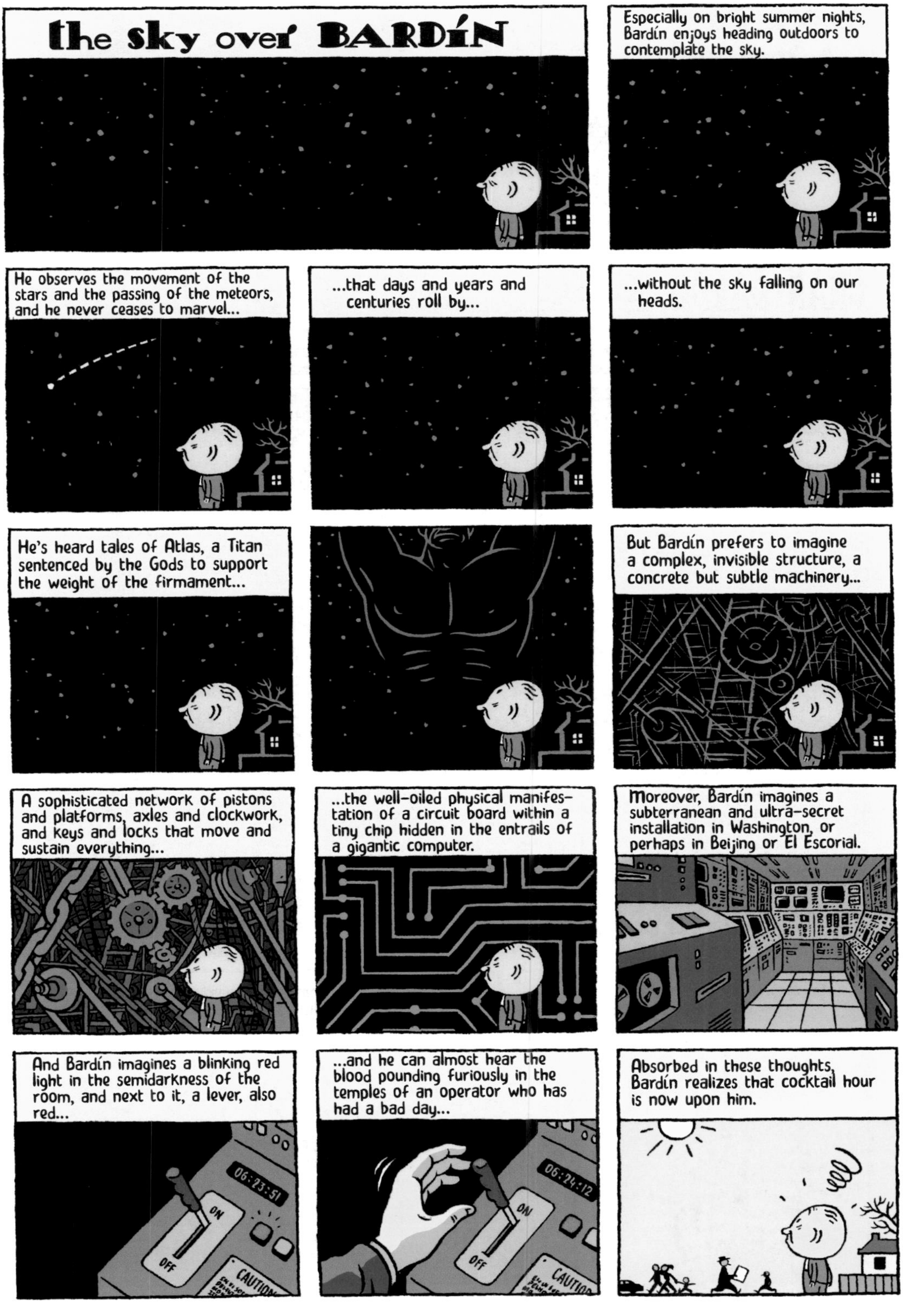
the sky over BARDÍN
Especially on bright summer nights, Bardín enjoys heading outdoors to contemplate the sky.
He observes the movement of the stars and the passing of the meteors, and he never ceases to marvel...
...that days and years and centuries roll by...
...without the sky falling on our heads.
He's heard tales of Atlas, a Titan sentenced by the Gods to support the weight of the firmament...
But Bardín prefers to imagine a complex, invisible structure, a concrete but subtle machinery...
A sophisticated network of pistons and platforms, axles and clockwork, and keys and locks that move and sustain everything...
...the well-oiled physical manifestation of a circuit board within a tiny chip hidden in the entrails of a gigantic computer.
Moreover, Bardín imagines a subterranean and ultra-secret installation in Washington, or perhaps in Beijing or El Escorial.
And Bardín imagines a blinking red light in the semidarkness of the room, and next to it, a lever, also red...
06:23:51
ON
OFF
CAUTION
...and he can almost hear the blood pounding furiously in the temples of an operator who has had a bad day...
06:24:12
ON
OFF
CAUTION
Absorbed in these thoughts, Bardín realizes that cocktail hour is now upon him.

homage to don luis buñuel

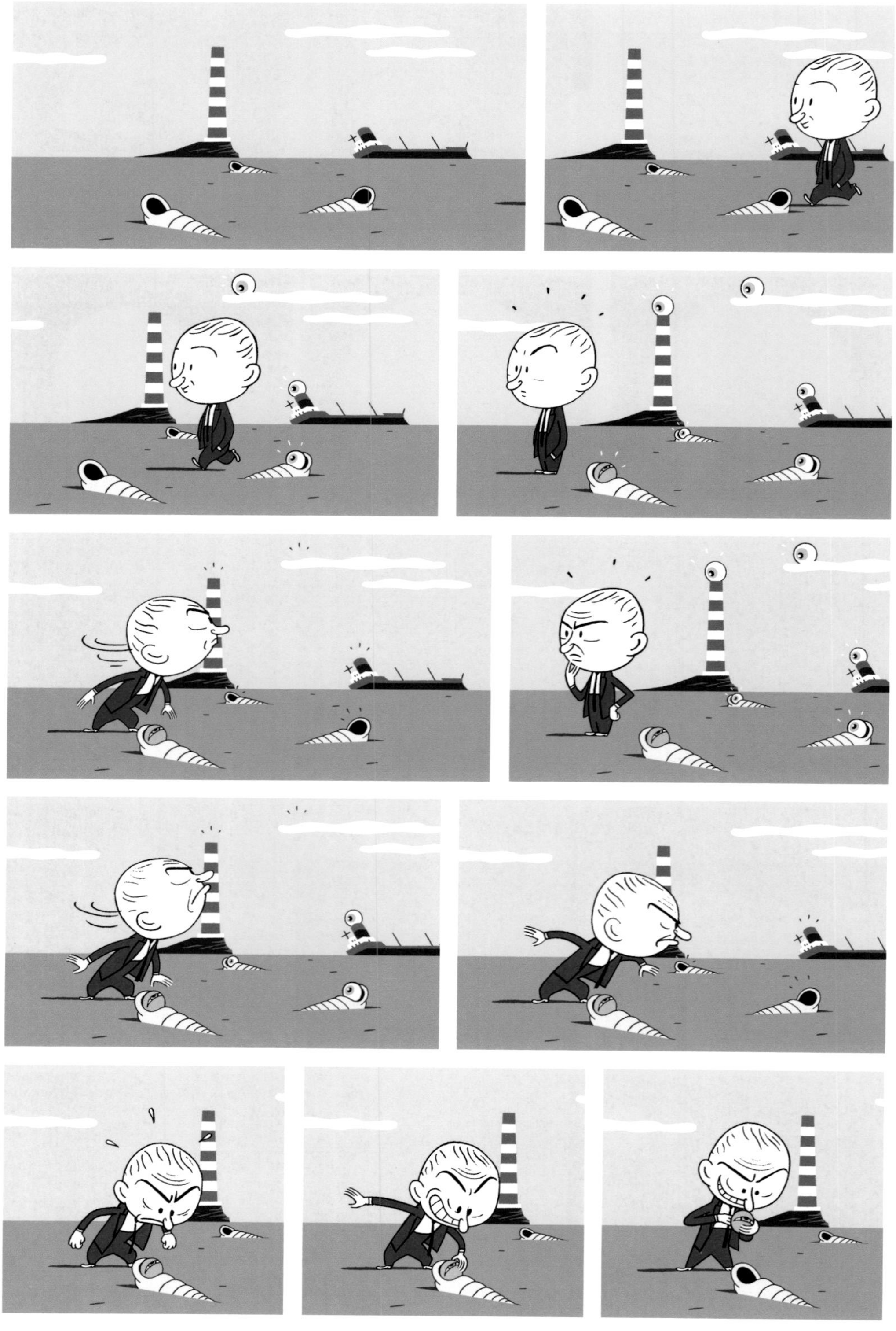

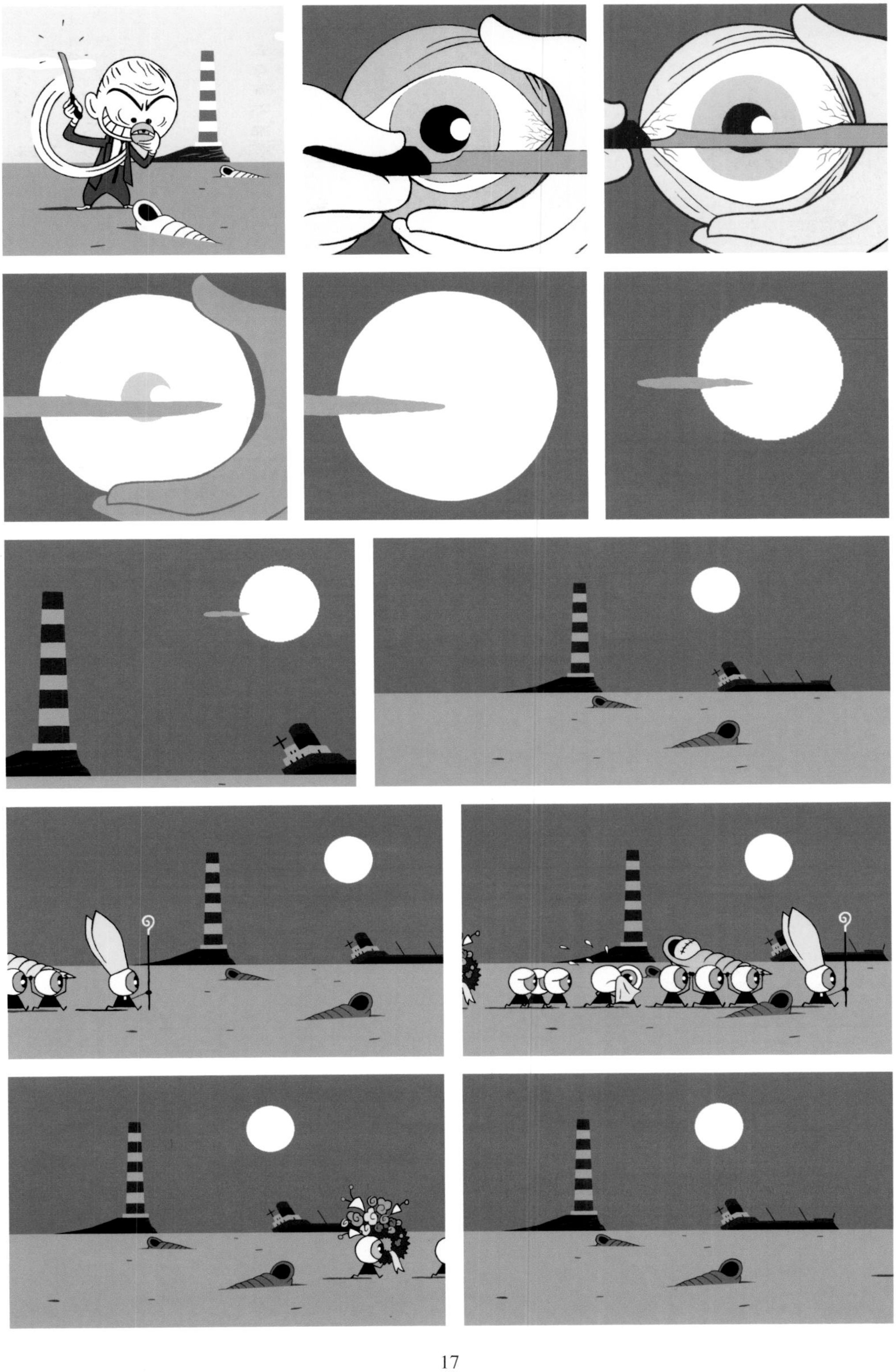

an act of love

Jesus!! Unbelievable!!

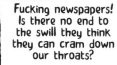

Fucking newspapers! Is there no end to the swill they think they can cram down our throats?

Feh! They must take us for retards!

pensión LOLITA

Café omercial

Hello there, Cirlot... What's got you so lost in thought?

Oh, nothing, just that these kids who're putting out a fanzine asked me to write an article for their tenth issue...

Tell me what you think: The art of drawing comics ennobles not only the practitioner, but also, to an ever greater degree, the reader who allows himself to be seduced by the mystery of transubstantiation of the drawn line into pure narrative. Steinberg said that he wrote with drawings. And it is in this spirit that...

Whoa, time out, guy! Where're you going with that musty old bullshit? Those kids're gonna laugh their asses off!

You think...?

Of course! Leave it to me, I'll hook you up with some fresh ideas! C'mon, buy me a cognac.

mumble... mmm... mumble mumble mumble!

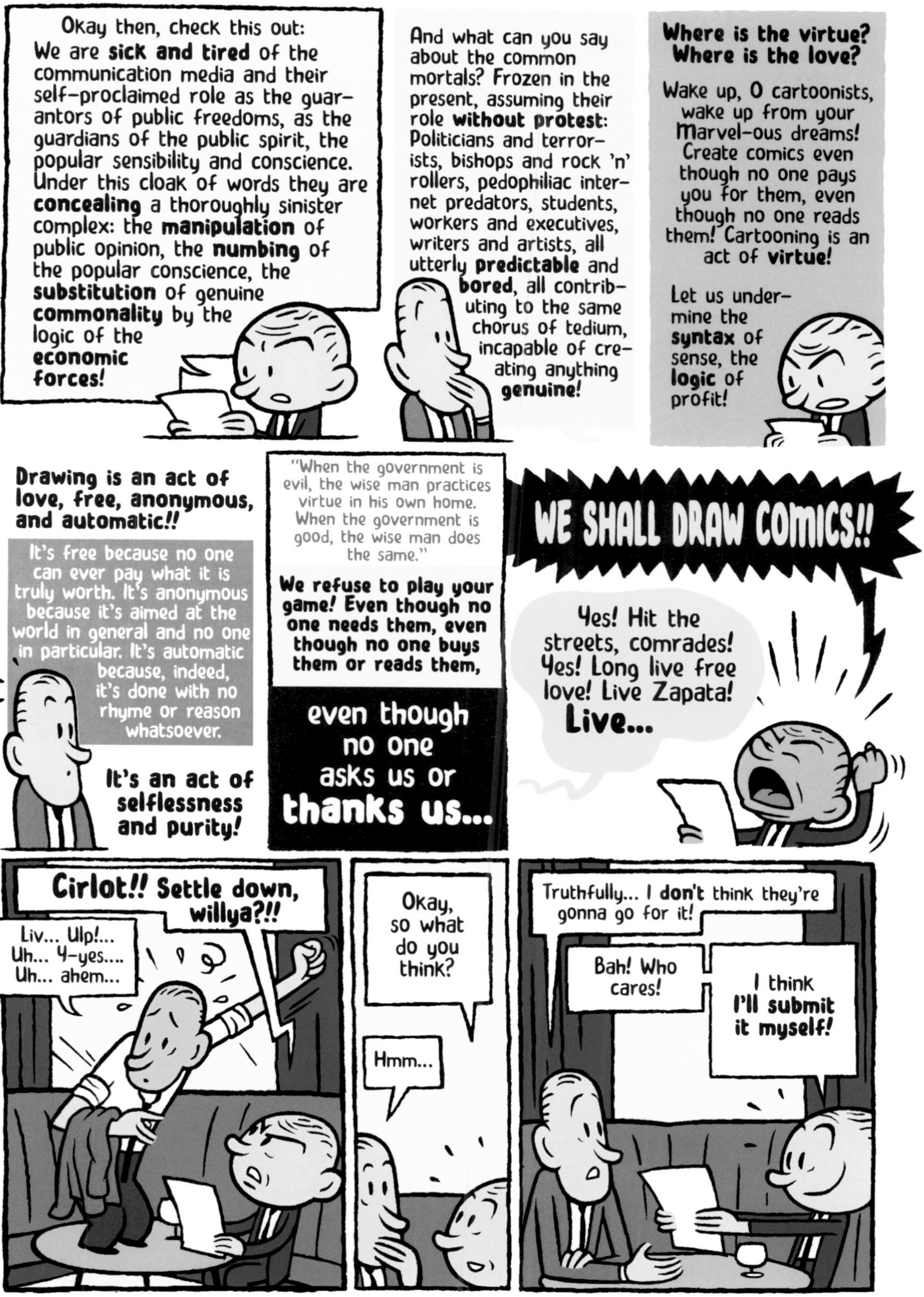
Okay then, check this out: We are sick and tired of the communication media and their self-proclaimed role as the guarantors of public freedoms, as the guardians of the public spirit, the popular sensibility and conscience. Under this cloak of words they are concealing a thoroughly sinister complex: the manipulation of public opinion, the numbing of the popular conscience, the substitution of genuine commonality by the logic of the economic forces!
And what can you say about the common mortals? Frozen in the present, assuming their role without protest: Politicians and terrorists, bishops and rock 'n' rollers, pedophiliac internet predators, students, workers and executives, writers and artists, all utterly predictable and bored, all contributing to the same chorus of tedium, incapable of creating anything genuine!
Where is the virtue? Where is the love?
Wake up, O cartoonists, wake up from your Marvel-ous dreams! Create comics even though no one pays you for them, even though no one reads them! Cartooning is an act of virtue!
Let us undermine the syntax of sense, the logic of profit!
Drawing is an act of love, free, anonymous, and automatic!!
It's free because no one can ever pay what it is truly worth. It's anonymous because it's aimed at the world in general and no one in particular. It's automatic because, indeed, it's done with no rhyme or reason whatsoever.
It's an act of selflessness and purity!
"When the government is evil, the wise man practices virtue in his own home. When the government is good, the wise man does the same."
We refuse to play your game! Even though no one needs them, even though no one buys them or reads them,
even though no one asks us or thanks us...
WE SHALL DRAW COMICS!!
Yes! Hit the streets, comrades! Yes! Long live free love! Live Zapata! Live...
Cirlot!! Settle down, willya?!!
Liv... Ulp!... Uh... Y-yes.... Uh... ahem...
Okay, so what do you think?
Hmm...
Truthfully... I don't think they're gonna go for it!
Bah! Who cares!
I think I'll submit it myself!

nightmare no. 11

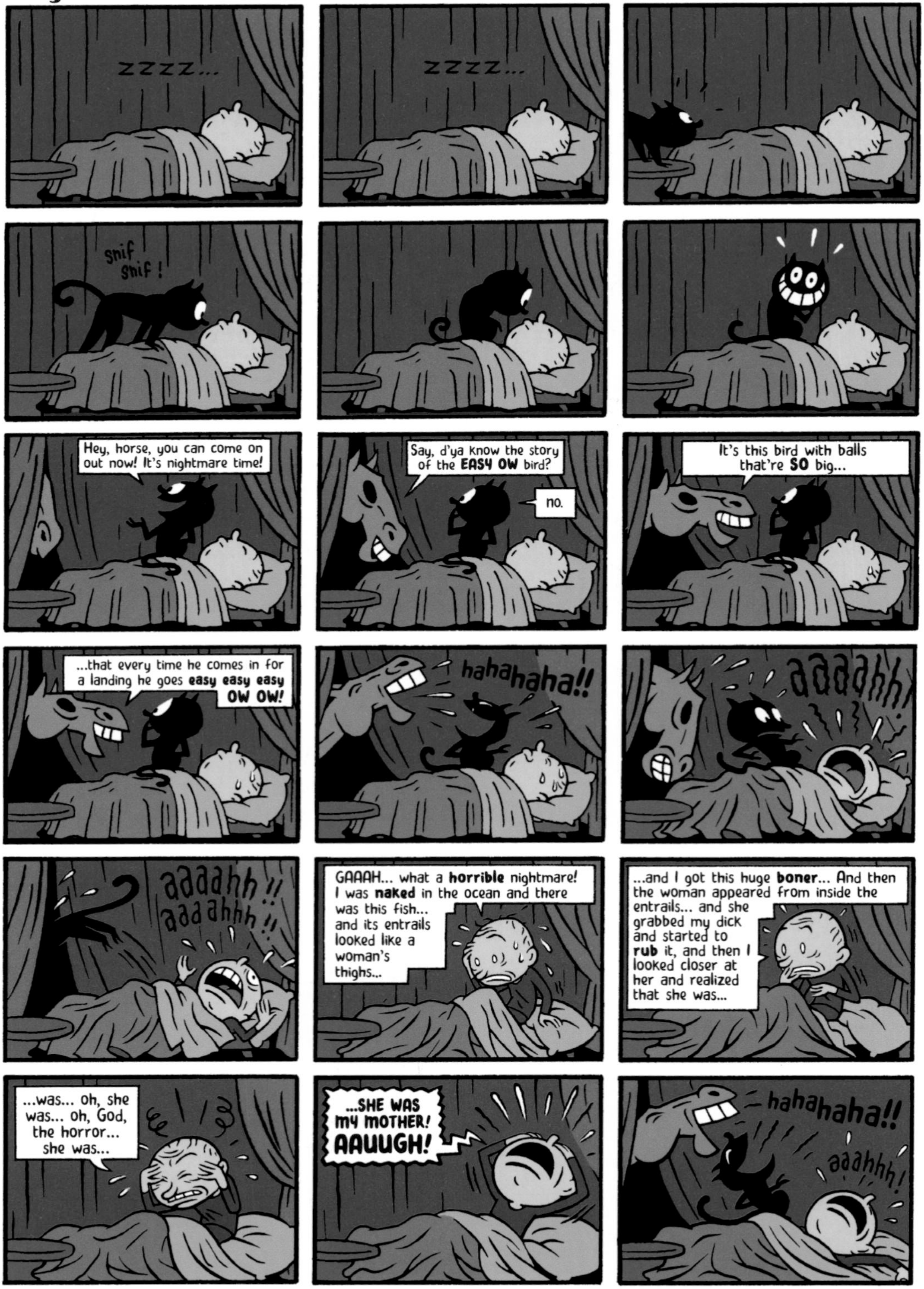

zzzz...
zzzz...
snif snif!
Hey, horse, you can come on out now! It's nightmare time!
Say, d'ya know the story of the EASY OW bird?
no.
It's this bird with balls that're SO big...
...that every time he comes in for a landing he goes easy easy easy OW OW!
hahahaha!!
aaaahhh
aaaahh!! aaaahhh!!
GAAAH... what a horrible nightmare! I was naked in the ocean and there was this fish... and its entrails looked like a woman's thighs...
...and I got this huge boner... And then the woman appeared from inside the entrails... and she grabbed my dick and started to rub it, and then I looked closer at her and realized that she was...
...was... oh, she was... oh, God, the horror... she was...
...SHE WAS MY MOTHER! AAUGH!
hahahaha!!
aaahhh!

the mysterious star

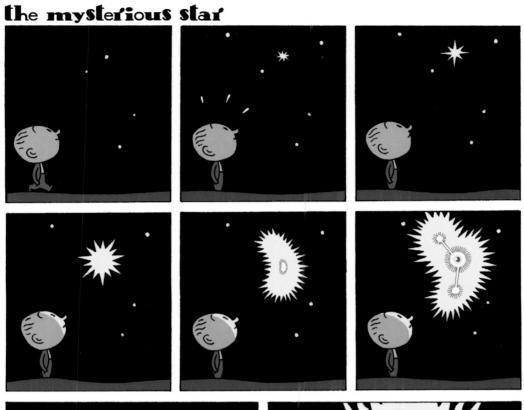

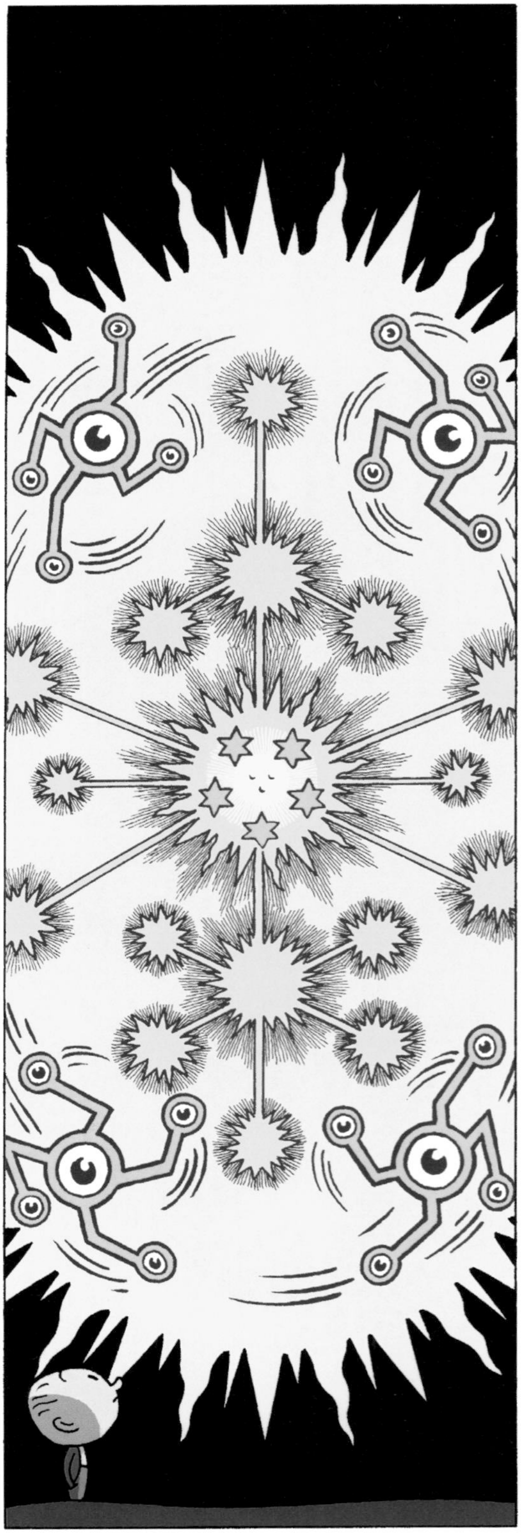
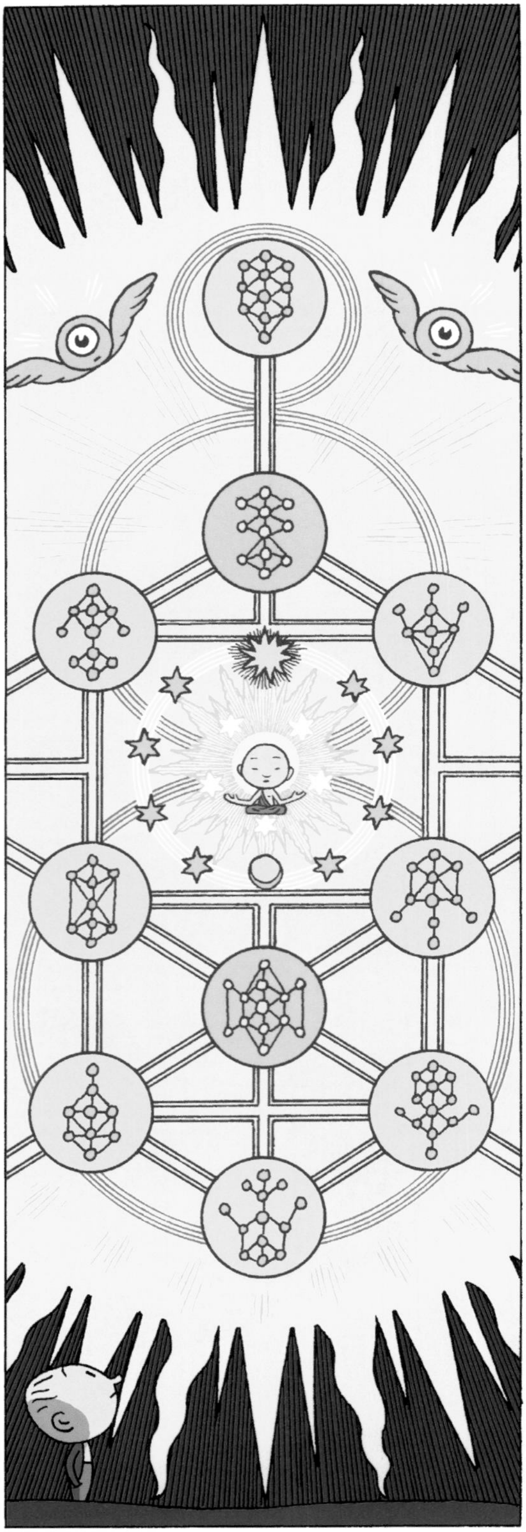

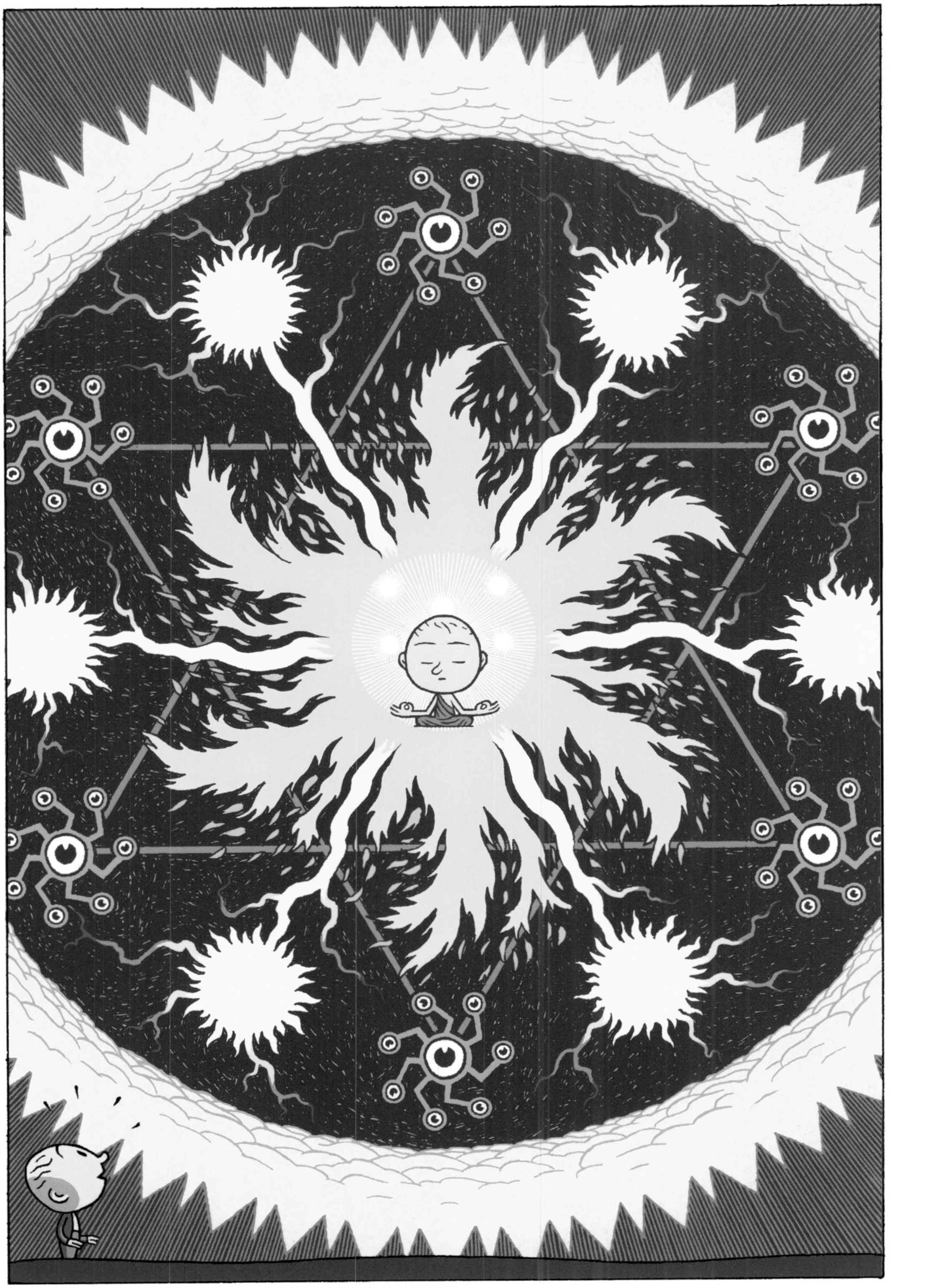

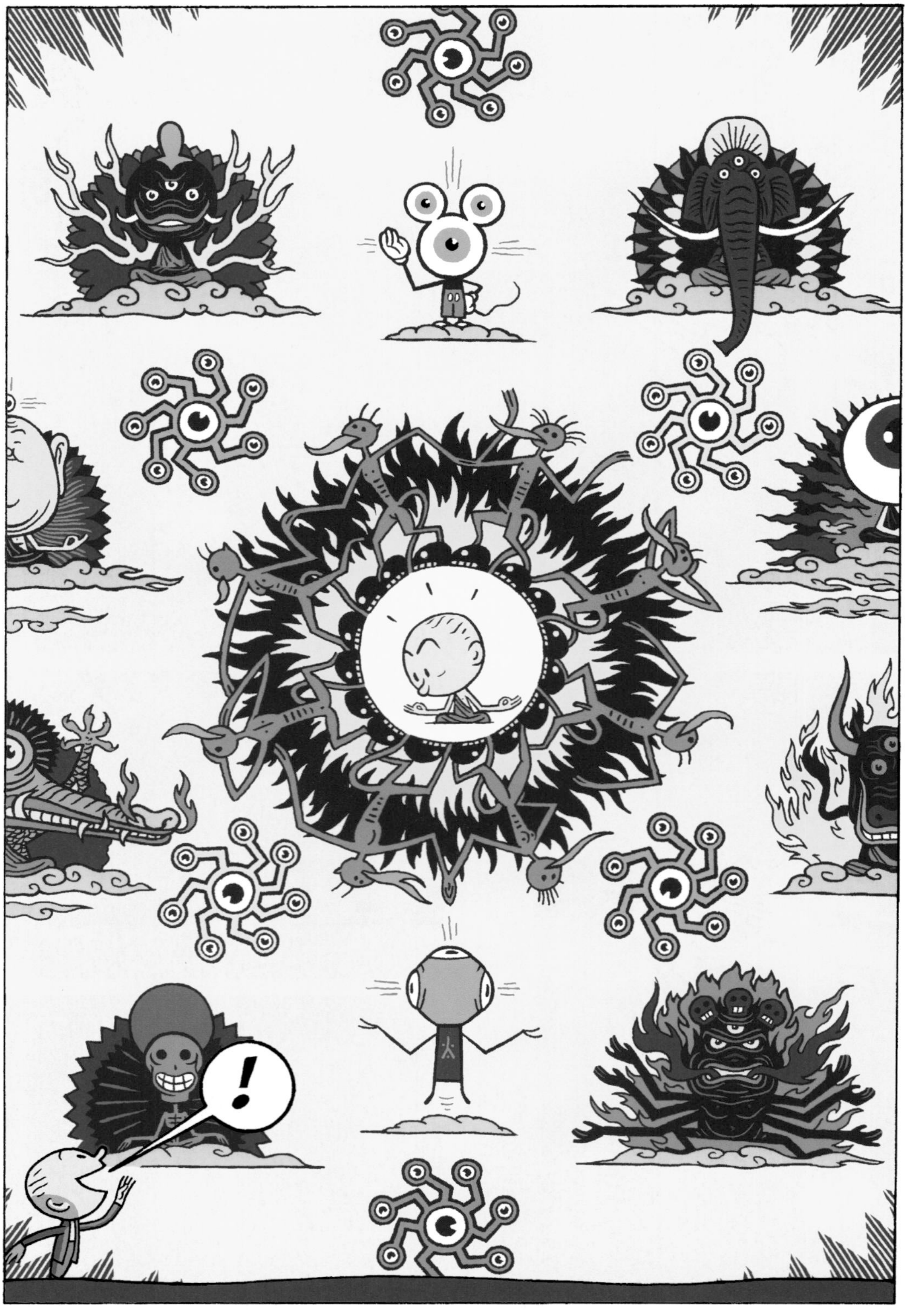
!

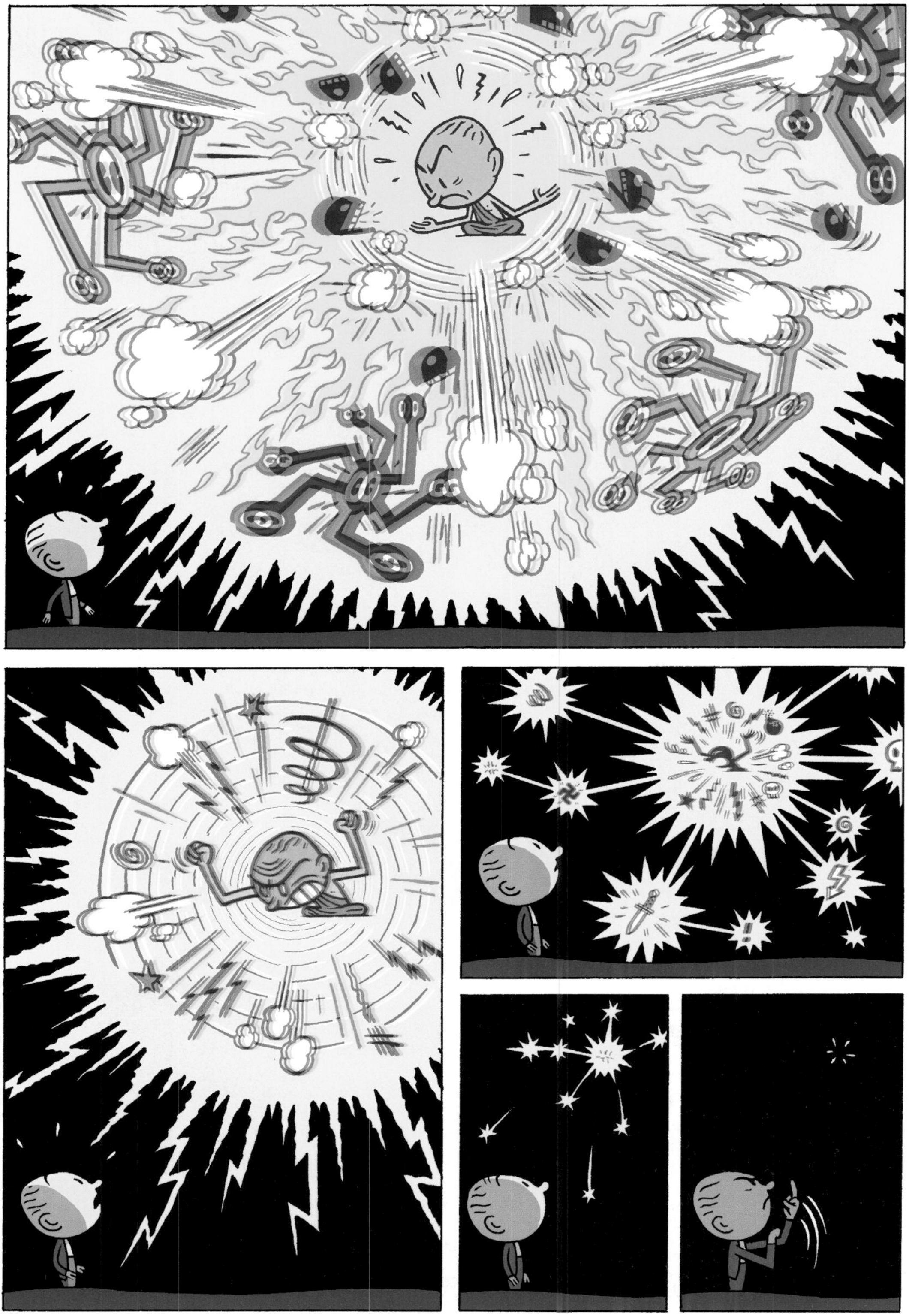

poet vs. poet

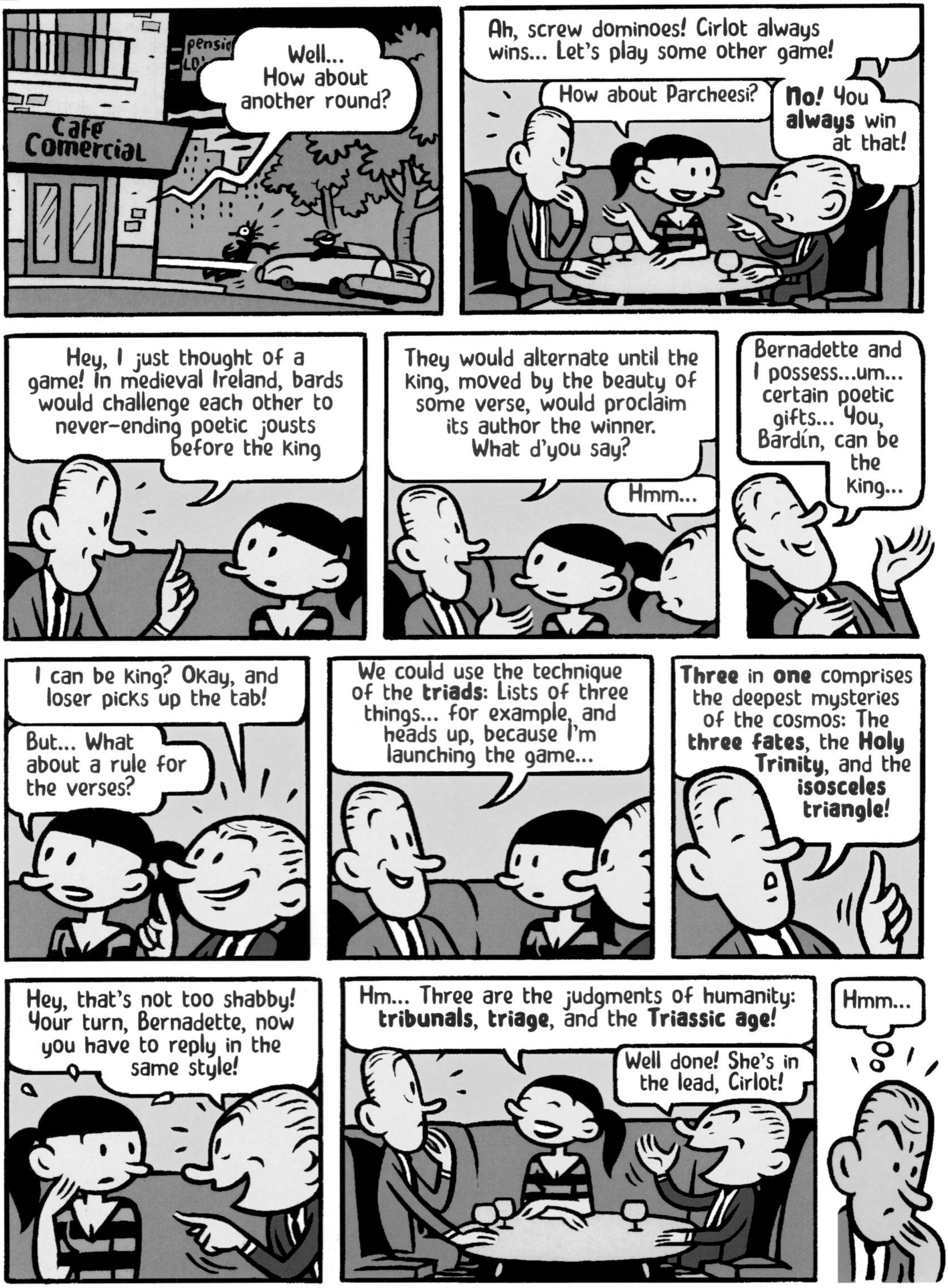

Café Comercial
Well... How about another round?
Ah, screw dominoes! Cirlot always wins... Let's play some other game!
How about Parcheesi?
No! You **always** win at that!
Hey, I just thought of a game! In medieval Ireland, bards would challenge each other to never-ending poetic jousts before the king
They would alternate until the king, moved by the beauty of some verse, would proclaim its author the winner. What d'you say?
Hmm...
Bernadette and I possess...um... certain poetic gifts... You, Bardín, can be the king...
I can be king? Okay, and loser picks up the tab!
But... What about a rule for the verses?
We could use the technique of the **triads**: Lists of three things... for example, and heads up, because I'm launching the game...
Three in **one** comprises the deepest mysteries of the cosmos: The **three fates**, the **Holy Trinity**, and the **isosceles triangle!**
Hey, that's not too shabby! Your turn, Bernadette, now you have to reply in the same style!
Hm... Three are the judgments of humanity: **tribunals**, **triage**, and the **Triassic age!**
Well done! She's in the lead, Cirlot!
Hmm...

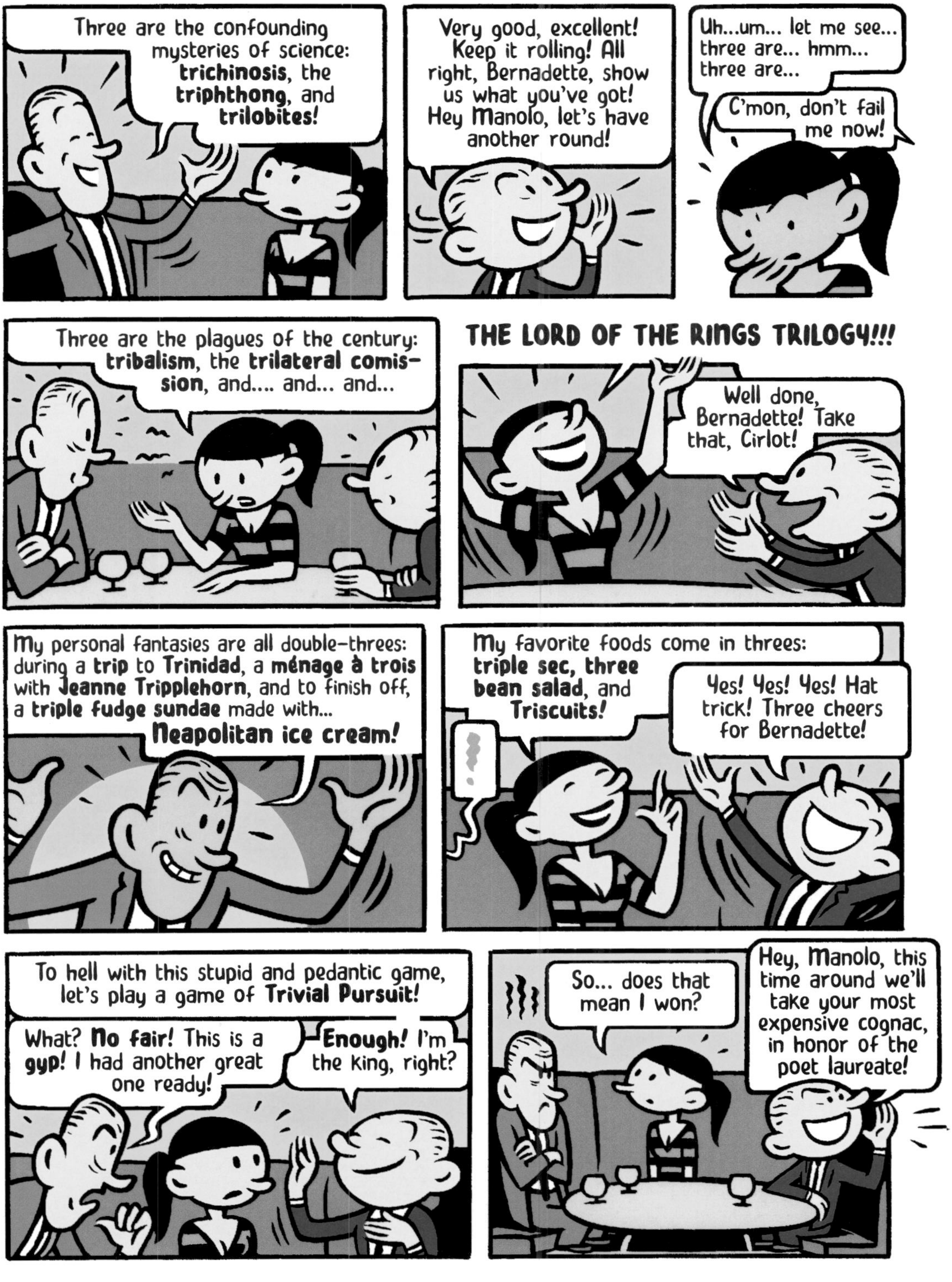
Three are the confounding mysteries of science: **trichinosis**, the **triphthong**, and **trilobites!**
Very good, excellent! Keep it rolling! All right, Bernadette, show us what you've got! Hey Manolo, let's have another round!
Uh...um... let me see... three are... hmm... three are...
C'mon, don't fail me now!
Three are the plagues of the century: **tribalism**, the **trilateral comis-sion**, and.... and... and...
THE LORD OF THE RINGS TRILOGY!!!
Well done, Bernadette! Take that, Cirlot!
My personal fantasies are all double-threes: during a **trip** to **Trinidad**, a **ménage à trois** with **Jeanne Tripplehorn**, and to finish off, a **triple fudge sundae** made with...
Neapolitan ice cream!
My favorite foods come in threes: **triple sec, three bean salad**, and **Triscuits!**
Yes! Yes! Yes! Hat trick! Three cheers for Bernadette!
To hell with this stupid and pedantic game, let's play a game of **Trivial Pursuit!**
What? **No fair!** This is a **gyp!** I had another great one ready!
Enough! I'm the king, right?
So... does that mean I won?
Hey, Manolo, this time around we'll take your most expensive cognac, in honor of the poet laureate!

Saint Ceremonio, Martyr

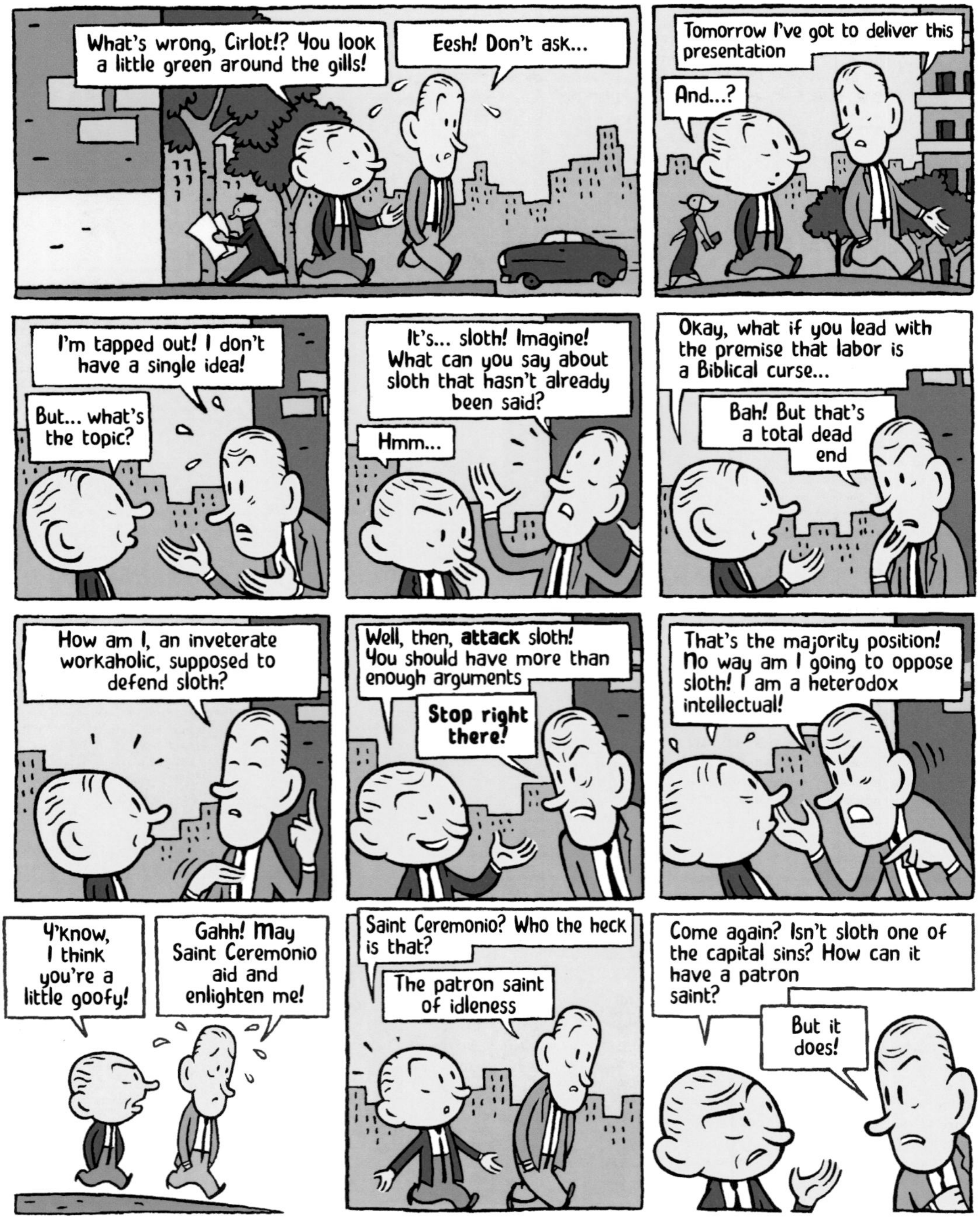
What's wrong, Cirlot!? You look a little green around the gills!
Eesh! Don't ask...
Tomorrow I've got to deliver this presentation
And...?
I'm tapped out! I don't have a single idea!
But... what's the topic?
It's... sloth! Imagine! What can you say about sloth that hasn't already been said?
Hmm...
Okay, what if you lead with the premise that labor is a Biblical curse...
Bah! But that's a total dead end
How am I, an inveterate workaholic, supposed to defend sloth?
Well, then, attack sloth! You should have more than enough arguments
Stop right there!
That's the majority position! No way am I going to oppose sloth! I am a heterodox intellectual!
Y'know, I think you're a little goofy!
Gahh! May Saint Ceremonio aid and enlighten me!
Saint Ceremonio? Who the heck is that?
The patron saint of idleness
Come again? Isn't sloth one of the capital sins? How can it have a patron saint?
But it does!

And most holy he is! If you don't believe me, check **this** out!

Wow! A saint card! Heh heh! Since when do you carry around saint cards in your pocket?

Hrmf...!

Anyway... want to hear his story or not?

Sure, but it's gotta be in front of two **cognacs**!

Ceremonio was originally a native of Asia Minor. Inflamed with missionary fervor by his conversion to Christianity, he traveled to Iberia in the year 64 in order to convert the Hispanics. But his sermons were so ponderous and his voice so monotonous that the few natives who approached to listen would nod off at his feet.

One day whilst the apostle was preaching by the seashore, he noticed that thousands of fish had gathered in the water, engrossed by his sermon. Deeply disappointed by the indifference of the humans, Ceremonio decided it would be a far better use of his time to convert the beasts of the sea.

But then the Hispanics, realizing what was going on, began to gather as well. Armed with staffs, they waded into the water and easily captured the finest specimens. Suddenly the locals' shabby diet was enriched with generous rations of lobster, salmon, sea bass, and turbot.

Thousands upon thousands of fish were massacred amid great tumult while Ceremonio, oblivious to it all, carried on with his lugubrious sermons. When the governor was apprised of the disturbances, he had the apostle seized and his tongue cut out.

Ceremonio returned to the beach to resume preaching, but the resultant guttural sounds and grotesque grimaces had no effect whatsoever on the fish, who dispersed as one. The Hispanics, enraged at having been deprived of their succulent rations, rained blows upon the apostle with their staffs and pitched him into the water, where he was devoured by the fish who evidently had thoroughly failed to absorb the godly message of his teachings.

It is said that Ceremonio, although frequently quite hungry, never in his life picked up a staff of his own with which to strike at the fish. From this was born the expression "like Ceremonio, you are not one to beat the waters," which as a comment on idleness has endured in the colloquial Spanish language to the present day.

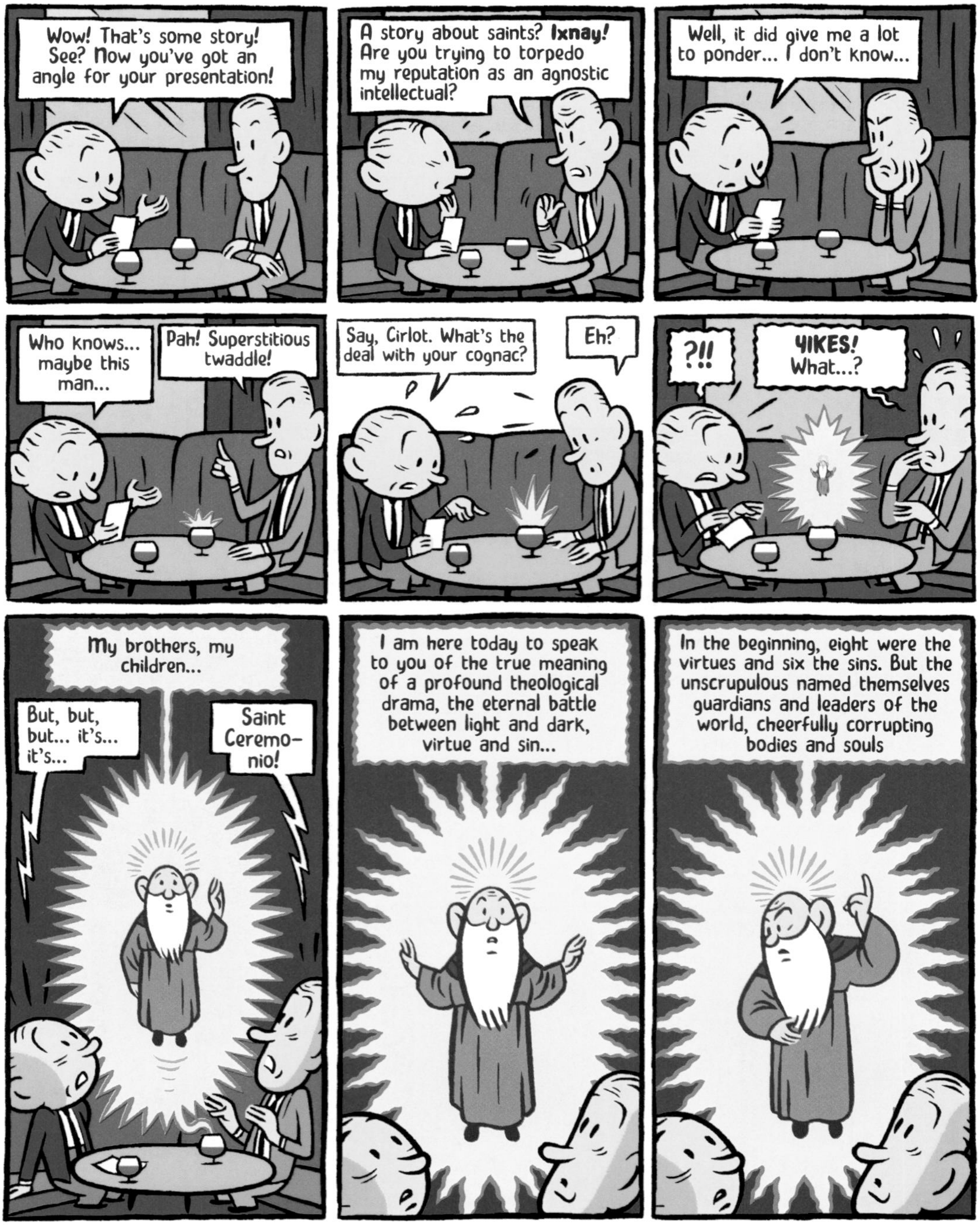

Wow! That's some story! See? Now you've got an angle for your presentation!
A story about saints? Ixnay! Are you trying to torpedo my reputation as an agnostic intellectual?
Well, it did give me a lot to ponder... I don't know...
Who knows... maybe this man...
Pah! Superstitious twaddle!
Say, Cirlot. What's the deal with your cognac?
Eh?
?!!
YIKES! What...?
My brothers, my children...
But, but, but... it's... it's...
Saint Ceremo-nio!
I am here today to speak to you of the true meaning of a profound theological drama, the eternal battle between light and dark, virtue and sin...
In the beginning, eight were the virtues and six the sins. But the unscrupulous named themselves guardians and leaders of the world, cheerfully corrupting bodies and souls

Such was the lamentable state of affairs, when one of the eight virtues decided to join her opposing numbers, bringing upon herself the scorn and loathing of her companions...

Sloth, that was the traitor's name

What they knew not was that she, carried by limitless selflessness and generosity, was sacrificing herself to the benefit of all

Indeed, Sloth had infiltrated the sins in order to destroy them from within!

Because consider this: **ANGER, PRIDE, GLUTTONY, ENVY, AVARICE** and **LUST**... Does not each of these, in order to be indulged, require a huge outlay of energy, a tremendous use of life force?

So you see, with sloth on their side they were fated to fade into smoke...

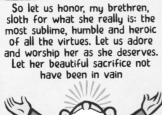

So let us honor, my brethren, sloth for what she really is: the most sublime, humble and heroic of all the virtues. Let us adore and worship her as she deserves. Let her beautiful sacrifice not have been in vain

Go with God, my children

A great truth!

There's no way around it!

We are virtu-ous! We are contending against sin!!

Let's go have a siesta!!

Okay, but first... another cognac?

You're on!

enlightenment

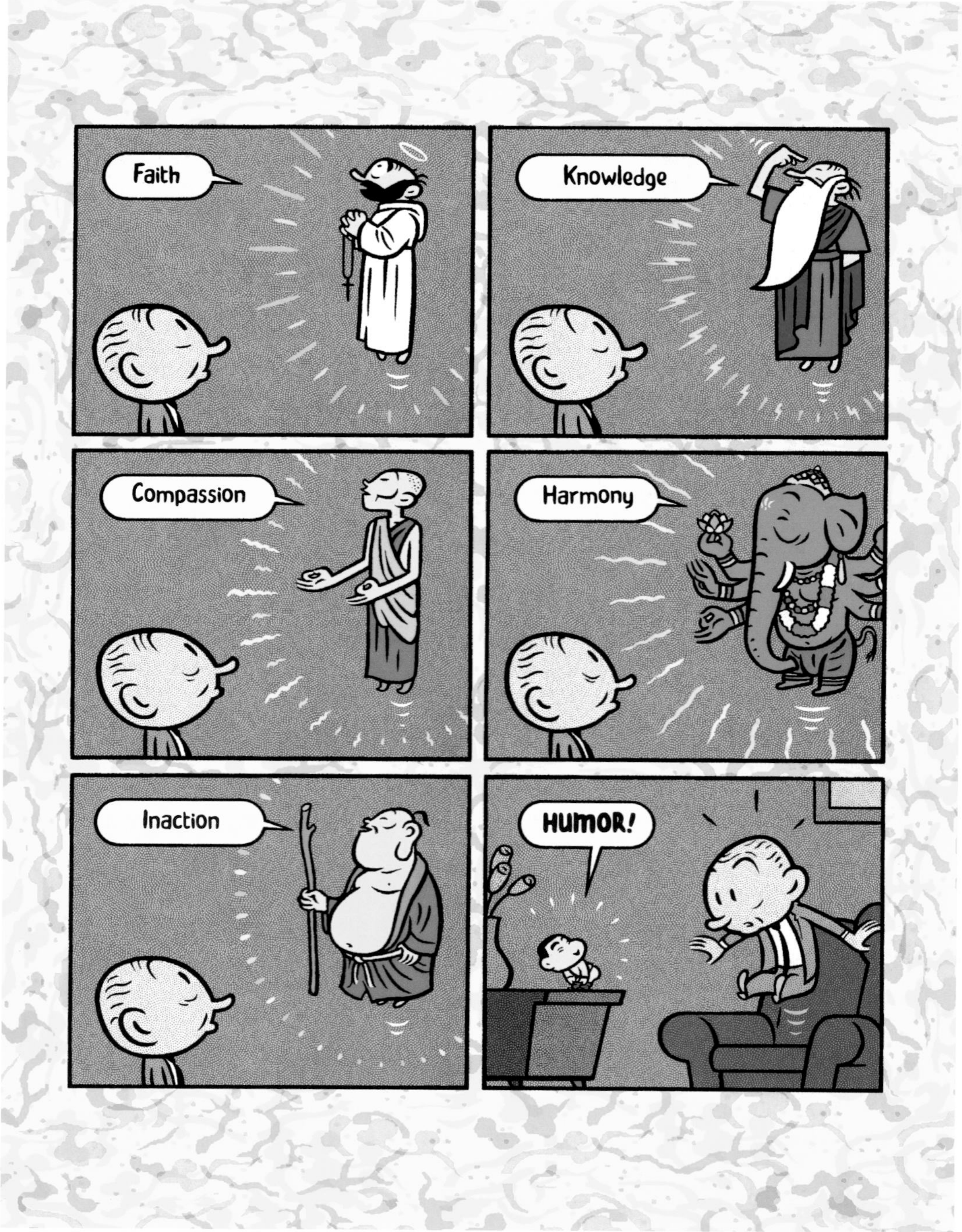
Faith
Knowledge
Compassion
Harmony
Inaction
HUMOR!

a metaphysical polemic

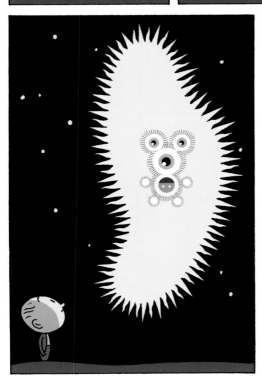

Greetings, O miserable and astonished **creature**. I find thee worthy, despite thy **puniness**, of infinite compassion!

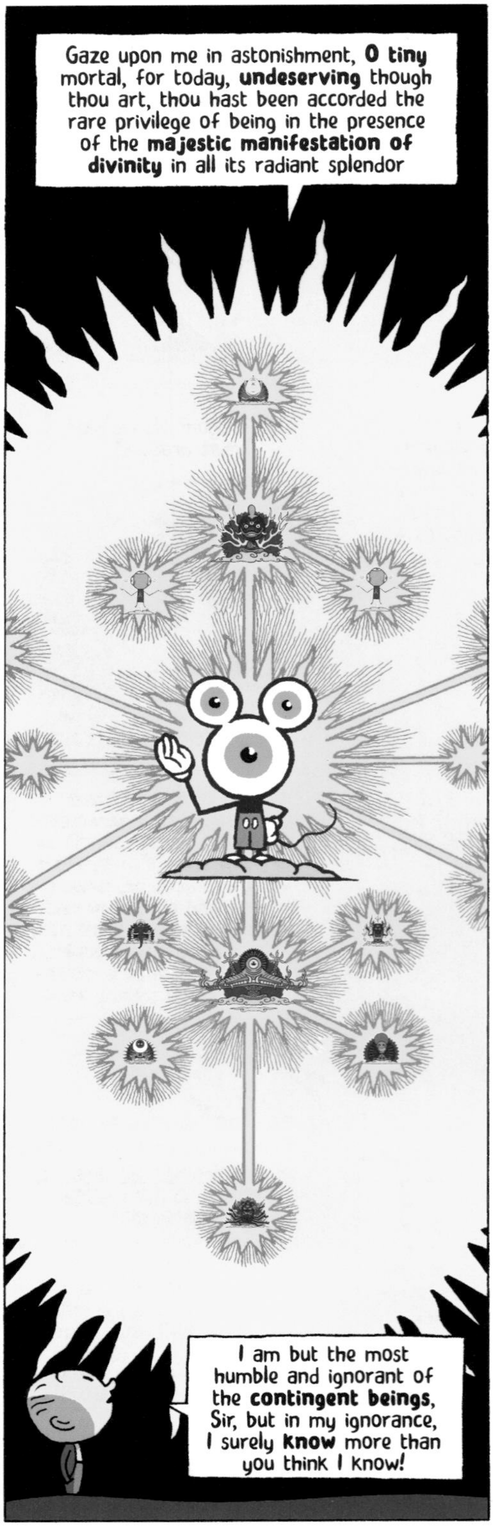
Gaze upon me in astonishment, **O tiny** mortal, for today, **undeserving** though thou art, thou hast been accorded the rare privilege of being in the presence of the **majestic manifestation of divinity** in all its radiant splendor
I am but the most humble and ignorant of the **contingent beings**, Sir, but in my ignorance, I surely **know** more than you think I know!

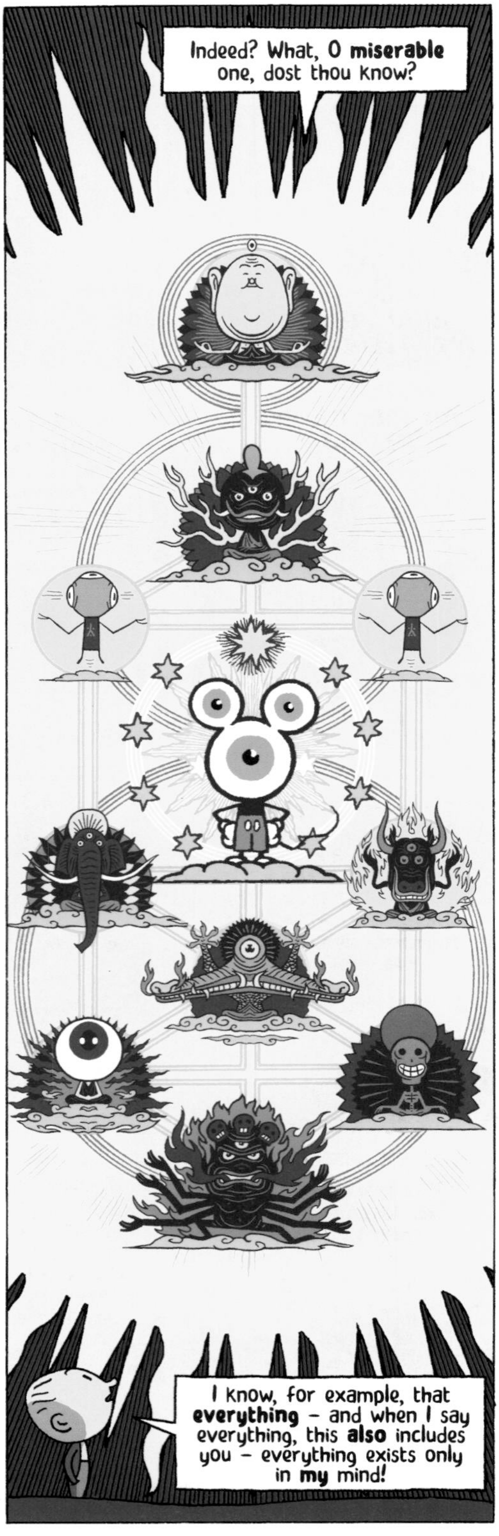
Indeed? What, O **miserable** one, dost thou know?
I know, for example, that **everything** – and when I say everything, this **also** includes you – everything exists only in **my** mind!

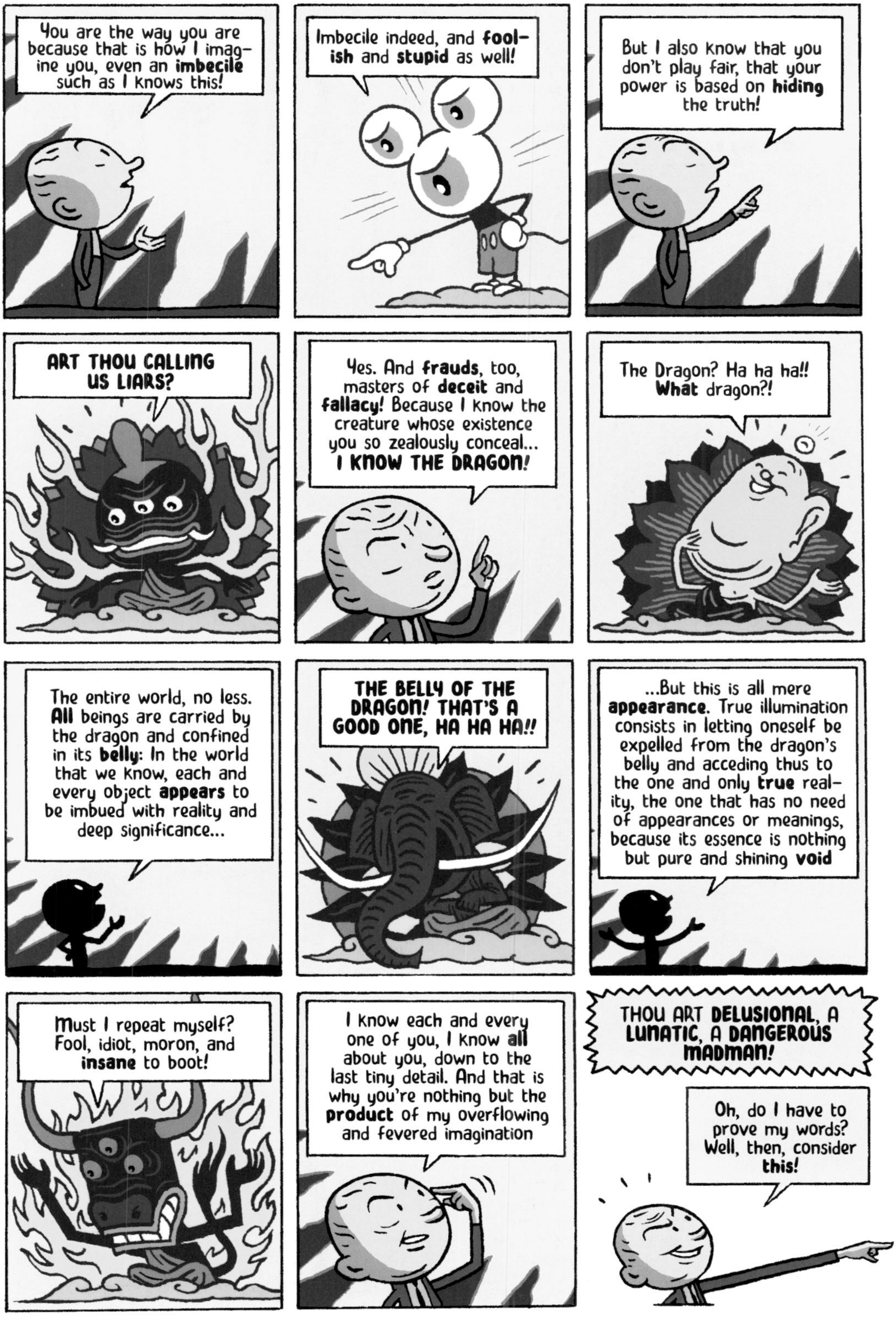
You are the way you are because that is how I imagine you, even an **imbecile** such as I knows this!
Imbecile indeed, and **foolish** and **stupid** as well!
But I also know that you don't play fair, that your power is based on **hiding** the truth!
ART THOU CALLING US LIARS?
Yes. And **frauds**, too, masters of **deceit** and **fallacy**! Because I know the creature whose existence you so zealously conceal... **I KNOW THE DRAGON!**
The Dragon? Ha ha ha!! **What** dragon?!
The entire world, no less. **All** beings are carried by the dragon and confined in its **belly**: In the world that we know, each and every object **appears** to be imbued with reality and deep significance...
THE BELLY OF THE DRAGON! THAT'S A GOOD ONE, HA HA HA!!
...But this is all mere **appearance**. True illumination consists in letting oneself be expelled from the dragon's belly and acceding thus to the one and only **true** reality, the one that has no need of appearances or meanings, because its essence is nothing but pure and shining **void**
Must I repeat myself? Fool, idiot, moron, and **insane** to boot!
I know each and every one of you, I know **all** about you, down to the last tiny detail. And that is why you're nothing but the **product** of my overflowing and fevered imagination
THOU ART **DELUSIONAL**, A **LUNATIC**, A **DANGEROUS MADMAN**!
Oh, do I have to prove my words? Well, then, consider **this**!

the cosmological system of the superreal divinities

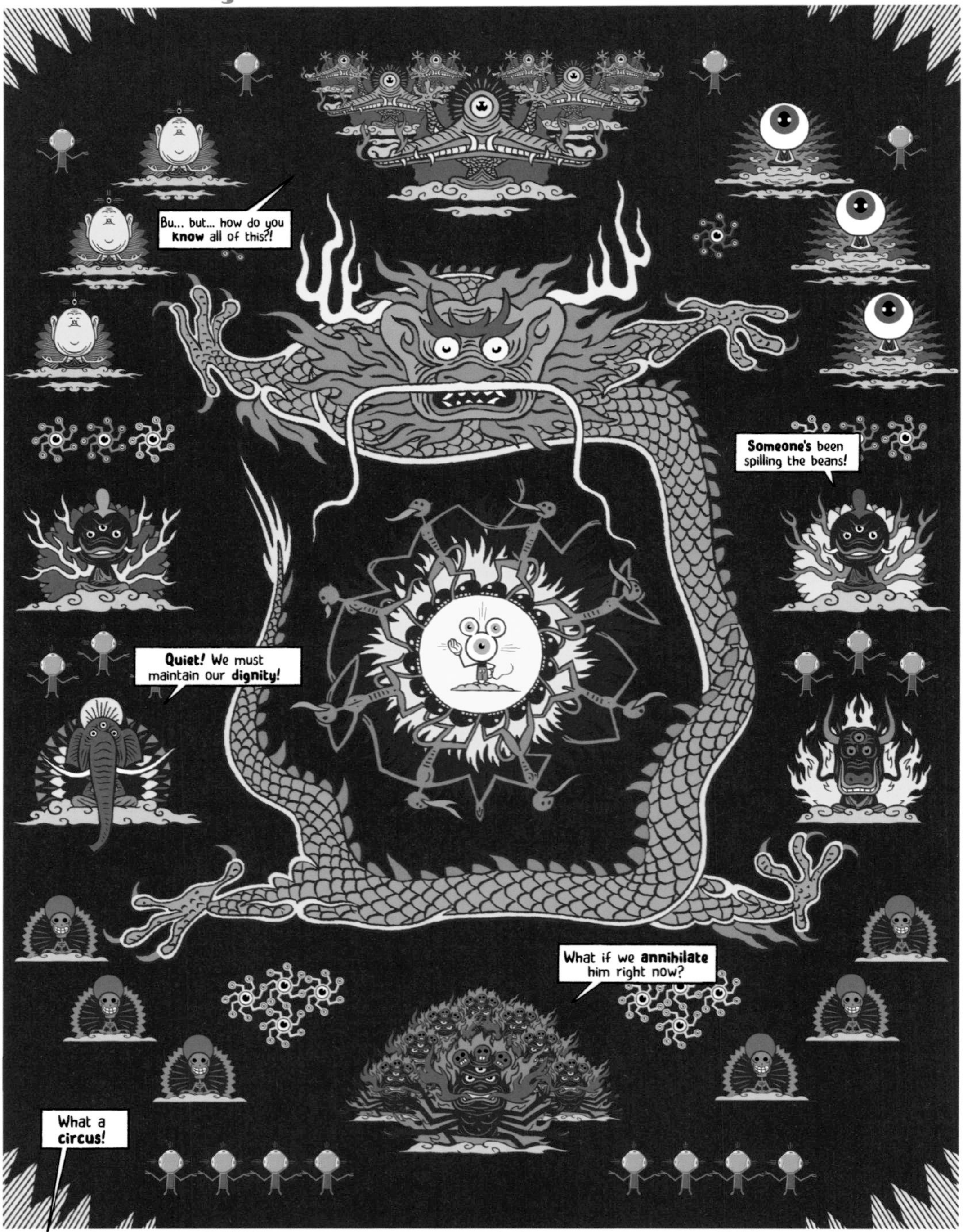

Bu... but... how do you **know** all of this?!
Someone's been spilling the beans!
Quiet! We must maintain our **dignity!**
What if we **annihilate** him right now?
What a **circus!**

In the center, the **ALIEN GOD** and the Wheel of the Eight Undeterrables. Surrounded in turn by the dragon **KI-NO**, in whose belly dwells the **GREAT SWINDLER**, who keeps all living beings subjugated to desire, passions, concupiscence and other calamities in order to justify the existence of a bewildering multitude of divinities. From left to right and top to bottom, **ONZO**, the benevolent Lord, Guardian of the Corners. **KRALA**, Mistress of the Flow of Time and Defender of the Crossroads. **SIRA**, the One Who Sees All But Understands Nothing, Guardian of the Faith. **SHOBA** (diurnal guise), Re-Adjuster of the Maladjusted. **SHOBA** (nocturnal guise), Punisher of Ignorance. **BACTANA**, Balm to the Conscience, Reconciler of Dreams. **VIC**, Divinity of Sexual Vigor and of Emergencies. **AVARDAVA**, Mistress of Illumination and Awakening, and her cohorts, Punishers of the Ego. **AVARMAR** the Wrathful God, Punisher of Slip-ups. Also, protective eyes and psychopompic demons in great profusion.

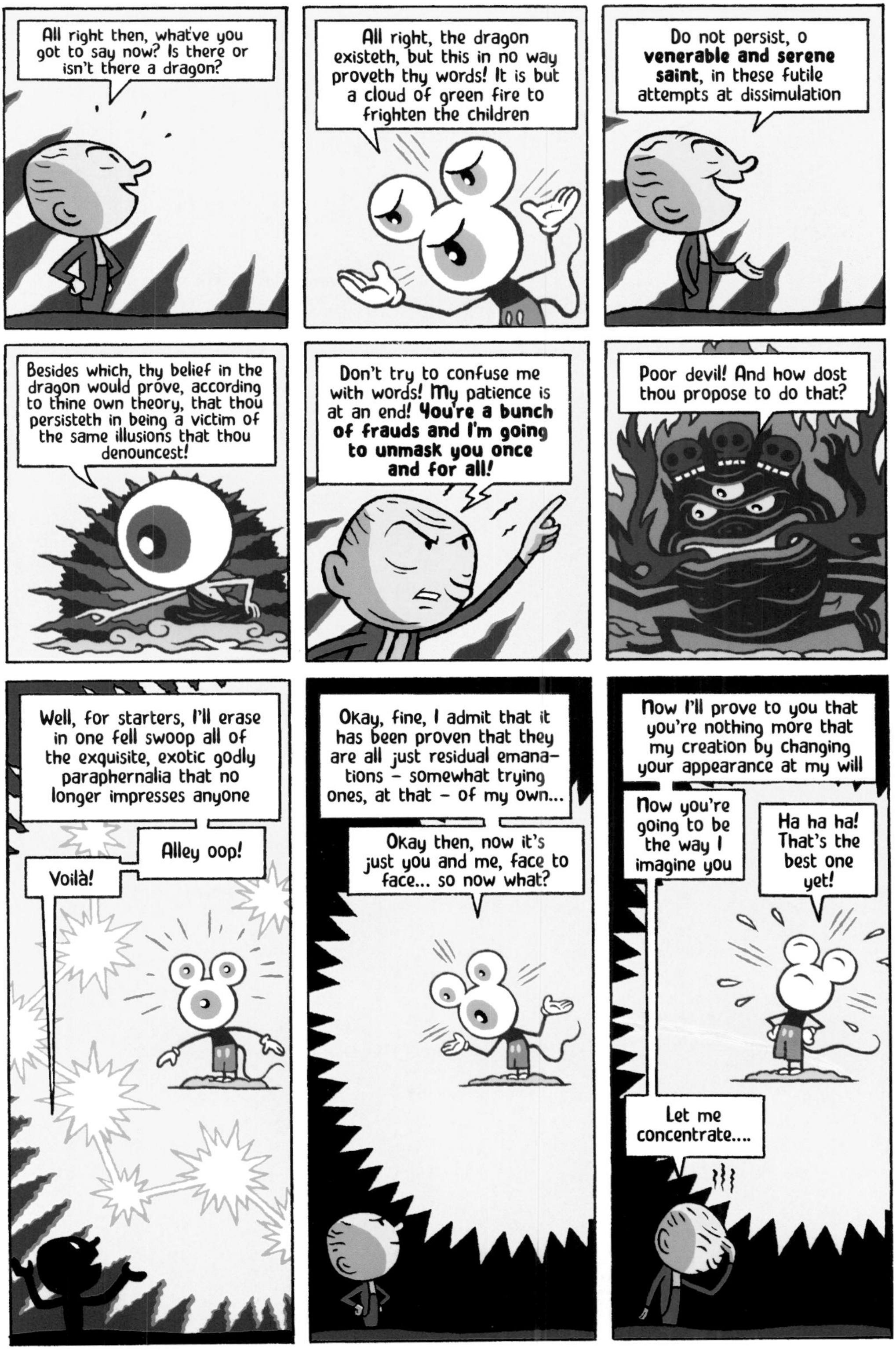

All right then, what've you got to say now? Is there or isn't there a dragon?
All right, the dragon existeth, but this in no way proveth thy words! It is but a cloud of green fire to frighten the children
Do not persist, o **venerable and serene saint**, in these futile attempts at dissimulation
Besides which, thy belief in the dragon would prove, according to thine own theory, that thou persisteth in being a victim of the same illusions that thou denouncest!
Don't try to confuse me with words! My patience is at an end! **You're a bunch of frauds and I'm going to unmask you once and for all!**
Poor devil! And how dost thou propose to do that?
Well, for starters, I'll erase in one fell swoop all of the exquisite, exotic godly paraphernalia that no longer impresses anyone
Alley oop!
Voilà!
Okay, fine, I admit that it has been proven that they are all just residual emanations – somewhat trying ones, at that – of my own...
Okay then, now it's just you and me, face to face... so now what?
Now I'll prove to you that you're nothing more that my creation by changing your appearance at my will
Now you're going to be the way I imagine you
Ha ha ha! That's the best one yet!
Let me concentrate....

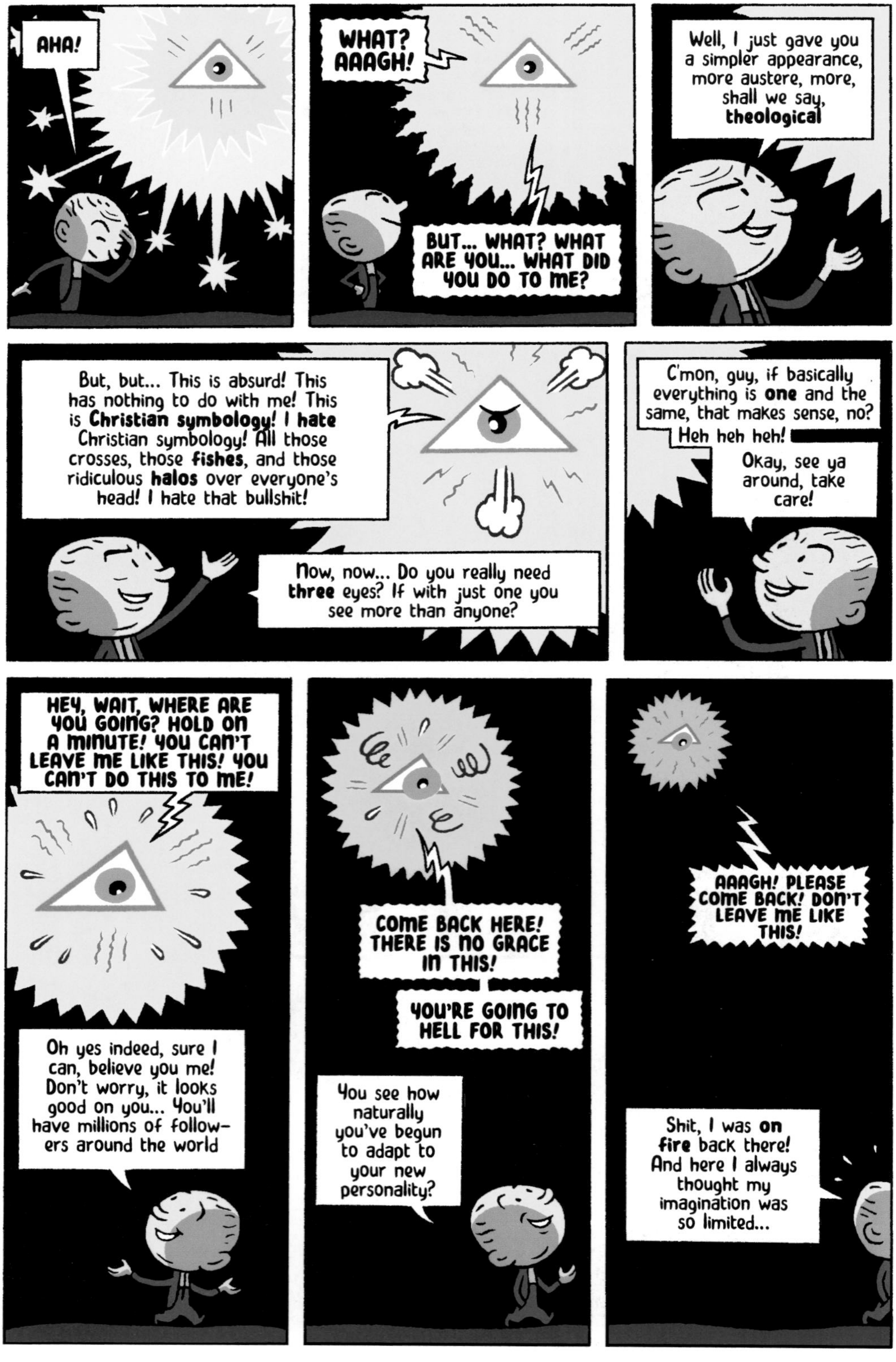
AHA!
WHAT? AAAGH!
BUT... WHAT? WHAT ARE YOU... WHAT DID YOU DO TO ME?
Well, I just gave you a simpler appearance, more austere, more, shall we say, theological
But, but... This is absurd! This has nothing to do with me! This is Christian symbology! I hate Christian symbology! All those crosses, those fishes, and those ridiculous halos over everyone's head! I hate that bullshit!
Now, now... Do you really need three eyes? If with just one you see more than anyone?
C'mon, guy, if basically everything is one and the same, that makes sense, no?
Heh heh heh!
Okay, see ya around, take care!
HEY, WAIT, WHERE ARE YOU GOING? HOLD ON A MINUTE! YOU CAN'T LEAVE ME LIKE THIS! YOU CAN'T DO THIS TO ME!
Oh yes indeed, sure I can, believe you me! Don't worry, it looks good on you... You'll have millions of follow-ers around the world
COME BACK HERE! THERE IS NO GRACE IN THIS!
YOU'RE GOING TO HELL FOR THIS!
You see how naturally you've begun to adapt to your new personality?
AAAGH! PLEASE COME BACK! DON'T LEAVE ME LIKE THIS!
Shit, I was on fire back there! And here I always thought my imagination was so limited...

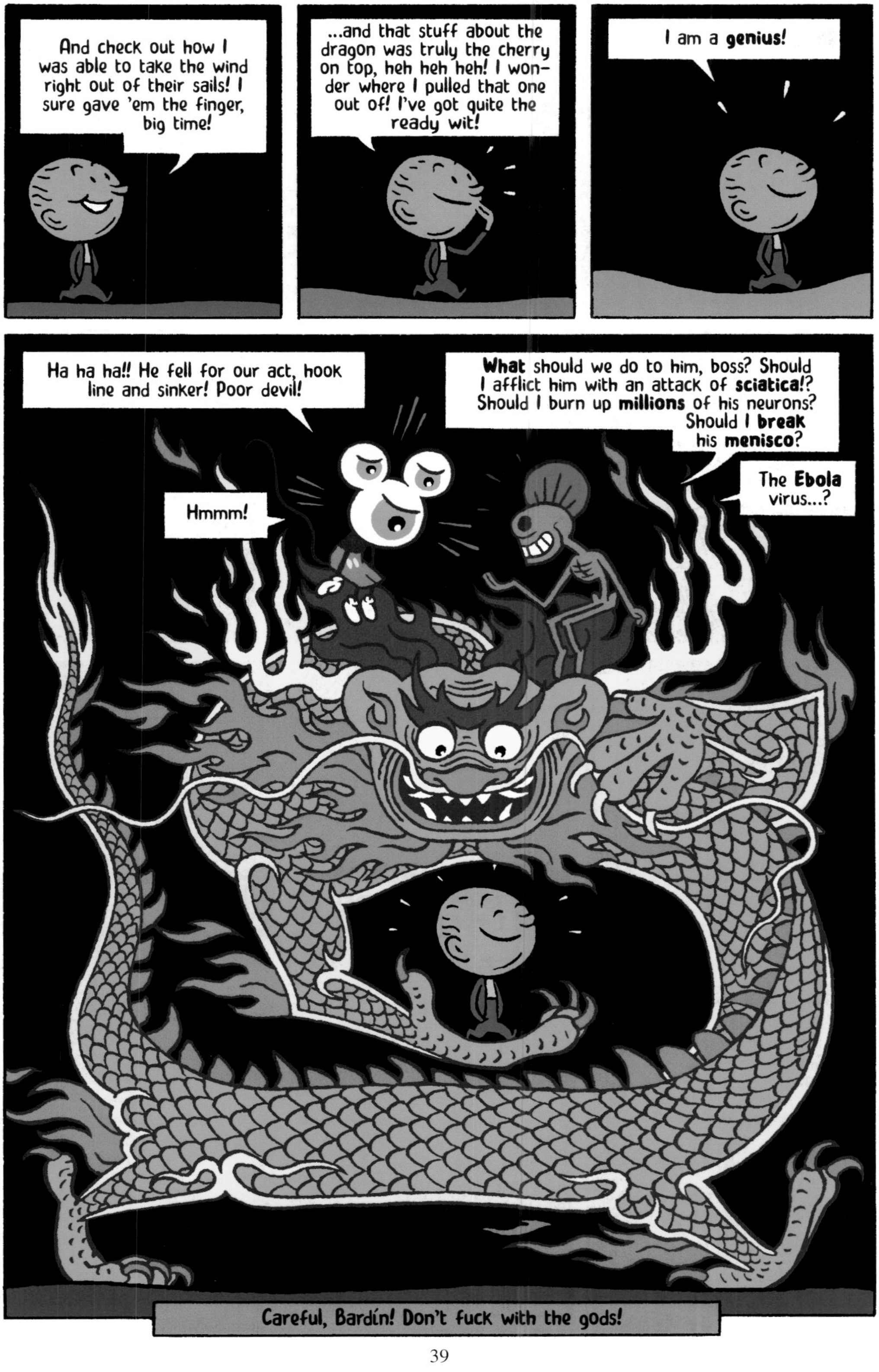

And check out how I was able to take the wind right out of their sails! I sure gave 'em the finger, big time!
...and that stuff about the dragon was truly the cherry on top, heh heh heh! I wonder where I pulled that one out of! I've got quite the ready wit!
I am a **genius!**
Ha ha ha!! He fell for our act, hook line and sinker! Poor devil!
Hmmm!
What should we do to him, boss? Should I afflict him with an attack of **sciatica!**? Should I burn up **millions** of his neurons? Should I **break** his **menisco**?
The **Ebola** virus...?
Careful, Bardín! Don't fuck with the gods!

nightmare no. 111

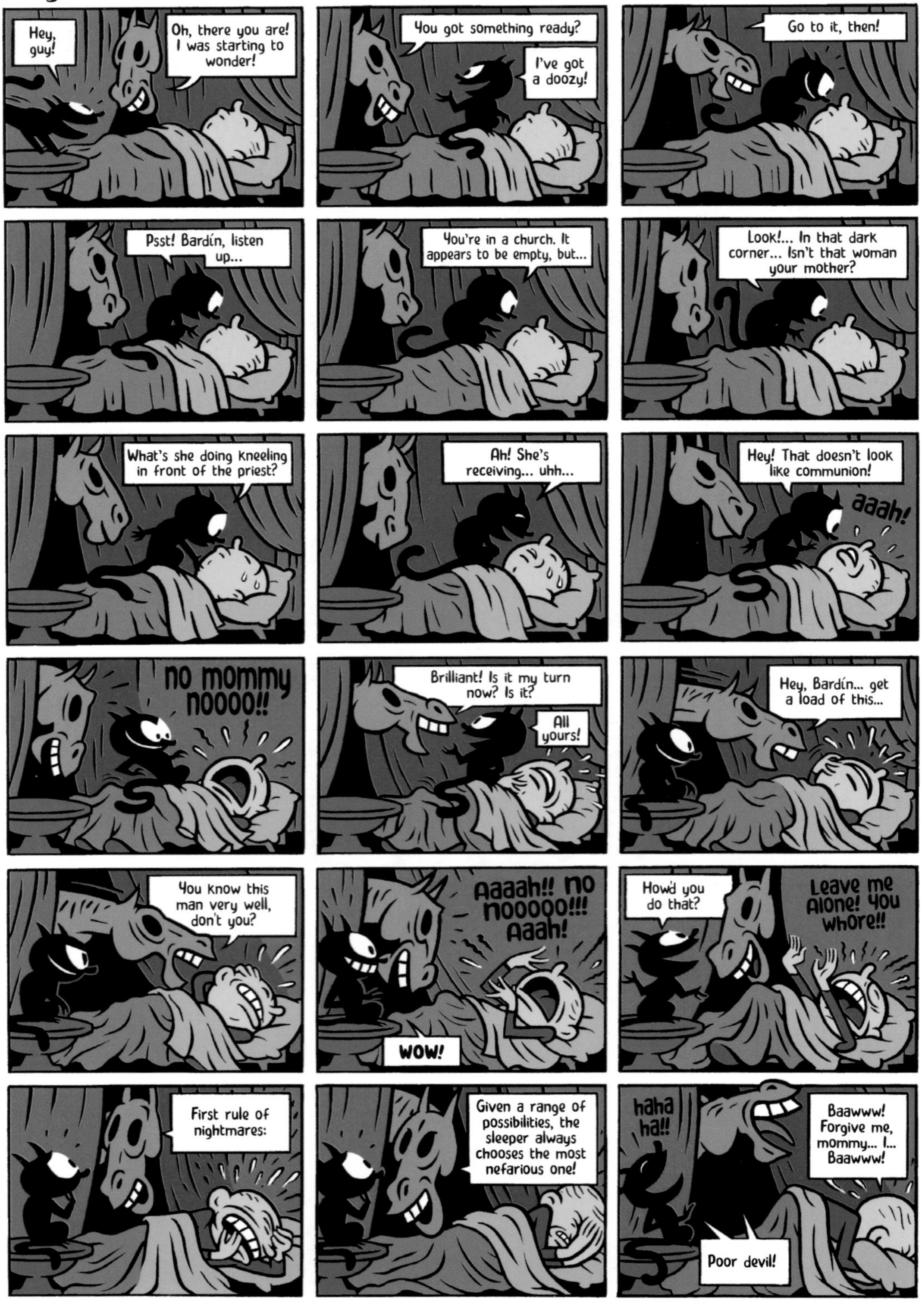

Hey, guy!
Oh, there you are! I was starting to wonder!
You got something ready?
I've got a doozy!
Go to it, then!
Psst! Bardín, listen up...
You're in a church. It appears to be empty, but...
Look!... In that dark corner... Isn't that woman your mother?
What's she doing kneeling in front of the priest?
Ah! She's receiving... uhh...
Hey! That doesn't look like communion!
aaah!
no mommy noooo!!
Brilliant! Is it my turn now? Is it?
All yours!
Hey, Bardín... get a load of this...
You know this man very well, don't you?
Aaaah!! no nooooo!!! Aaah!
WOW!
How'd you do that?
Leave me alone! You whore!!
First rule of nightmares:
Given a range of possibilities, the sleeper always chooses the most nefarious one!
haha ha!!
Baawww! Forgive me, mommy... I... Baawww!
Poor devil!

night-time stroll

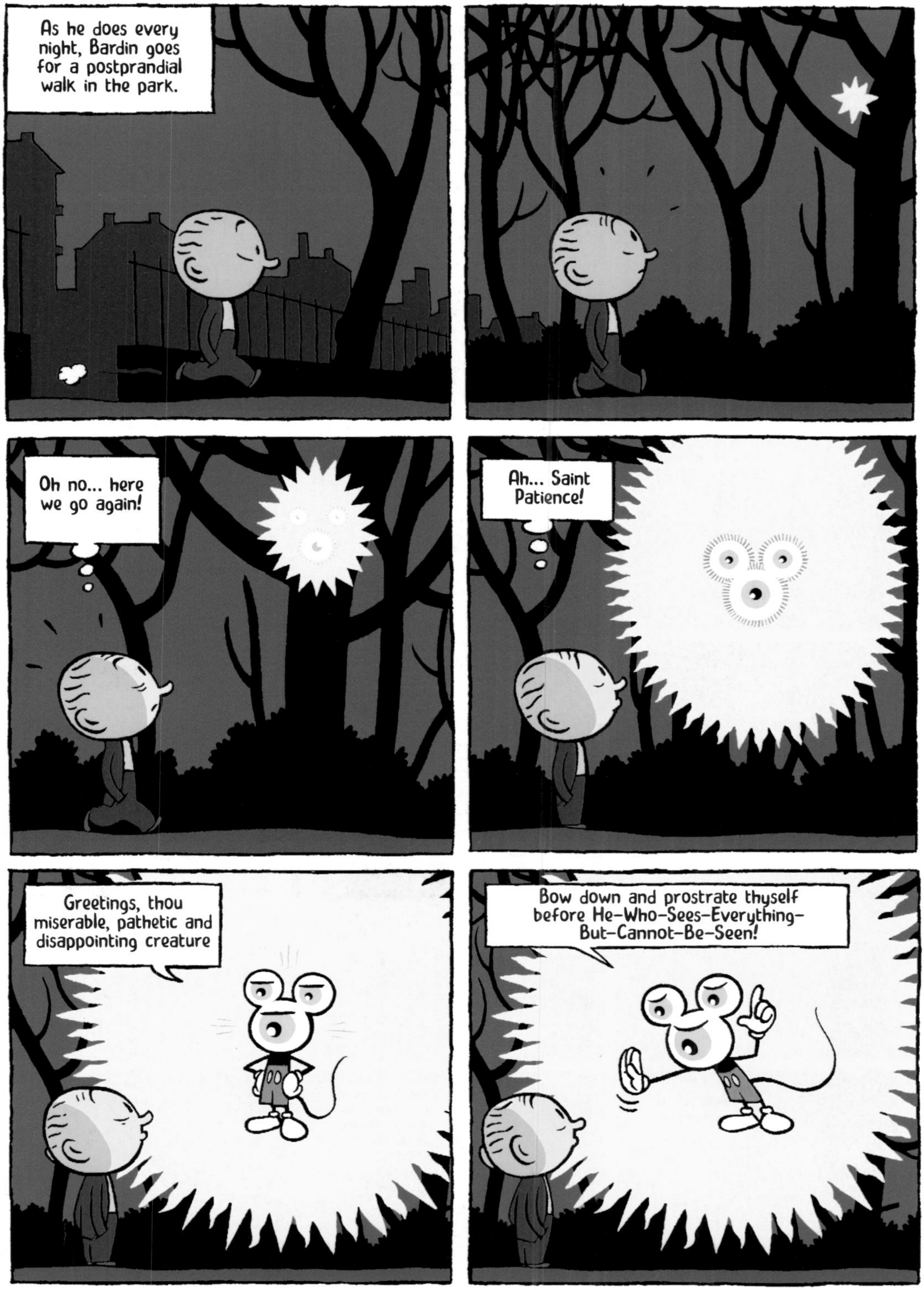

As he does every night, Bardin goes for a postprandial walk in the park.
Oh no... here we go again!
Ah... Saint Patience!
Greetings, thou miserable, pathetic and disappointing creature
Bow down and prostrate thyself before He-Who-Sees-Everything-But-Cannot-Be-Seen!

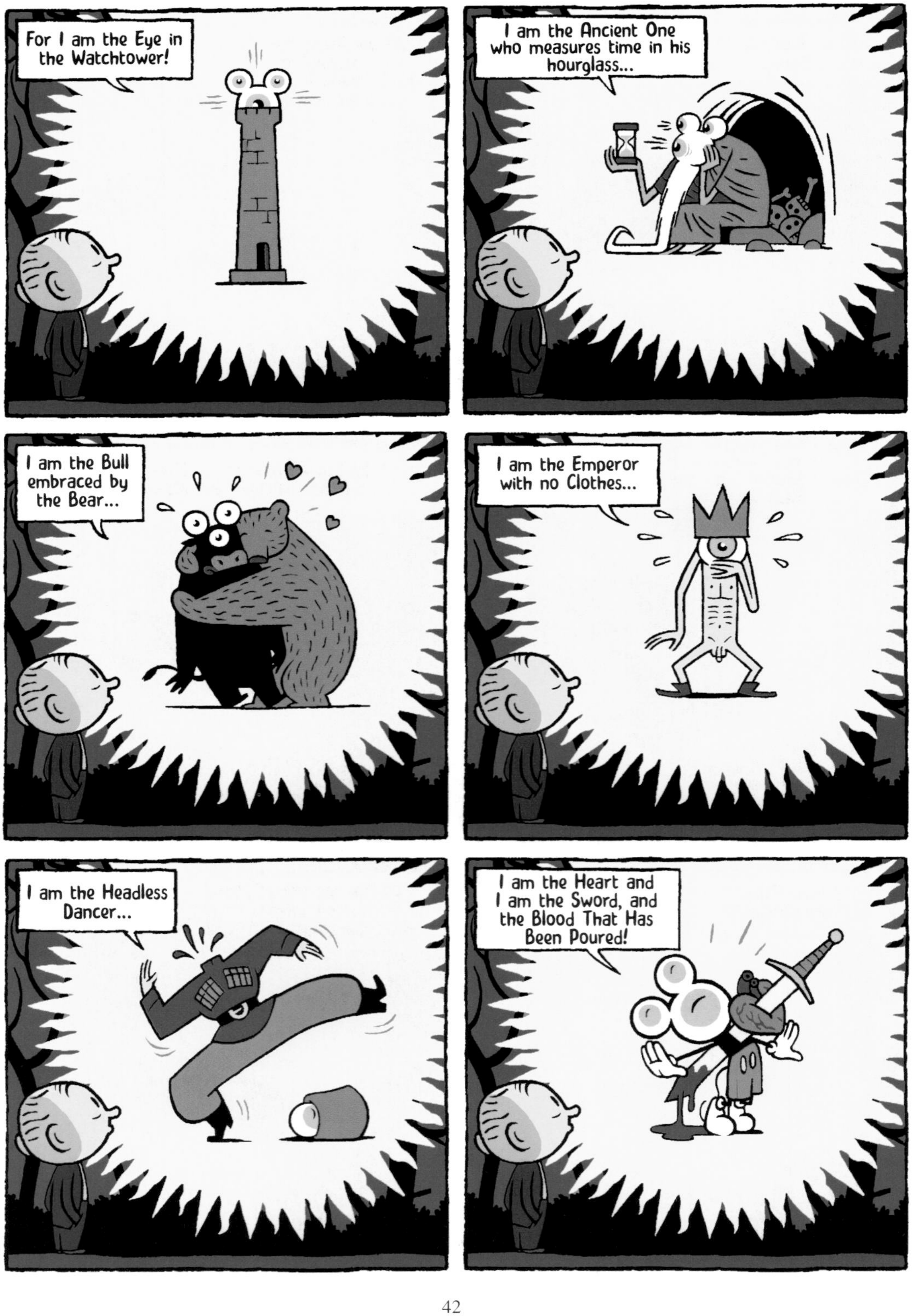
For I am the Eye in the Watchtower!
I am the Ancient One who measures time in his hourglass...
I am the Bull embraced by the Bear...
I am the Emperor with no Clothes...
I am the Headless Dancer...
I am the Heart and I am the Sword, and the Blood That Has Been Poured!

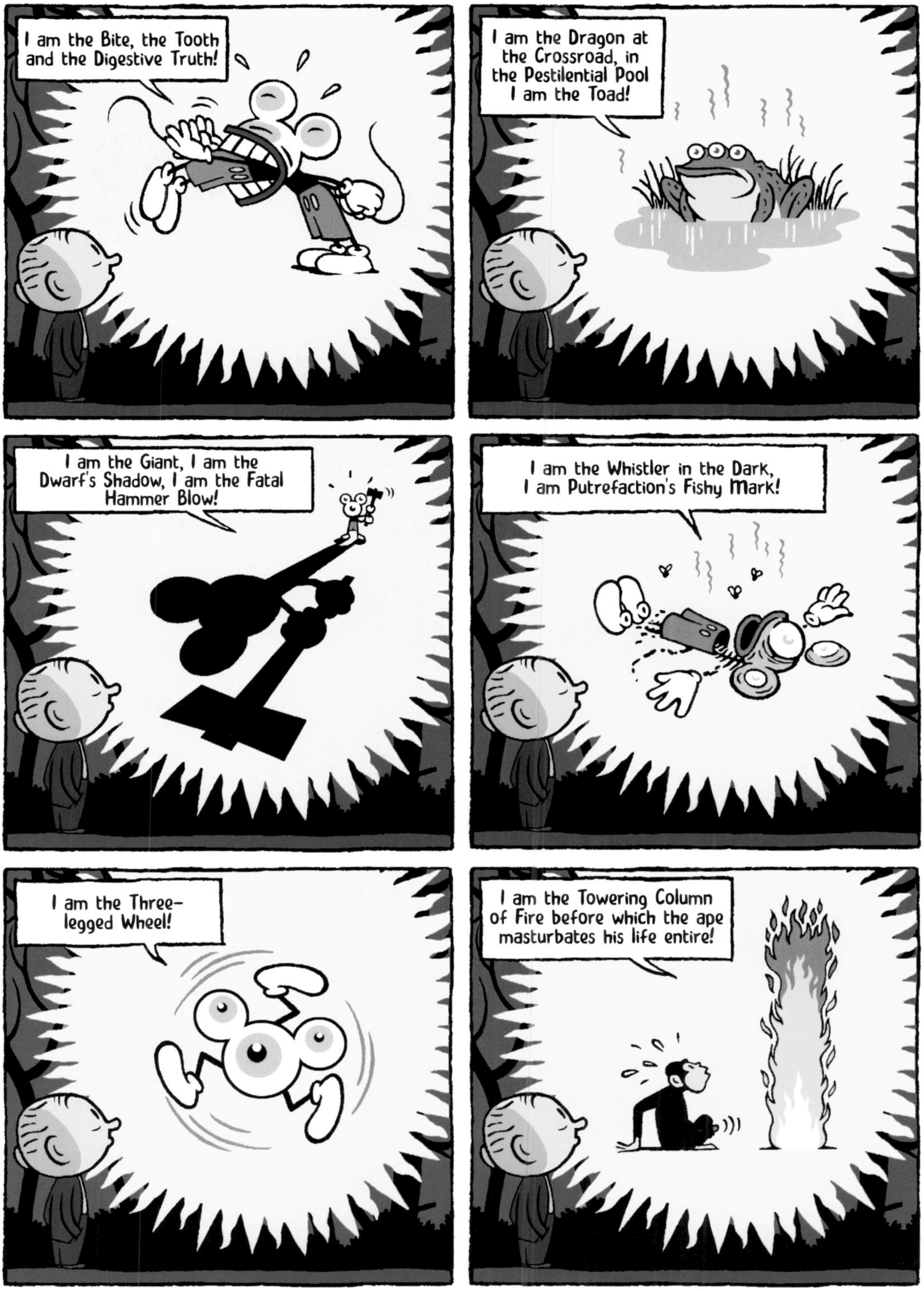

I am the Bite, the Tooth and the Digestive Truth!
I am the Dragon at the Crossroad, in the Pestilential Pool I am the Toad!
I am the Giant, I am the Dwarf's Shadow, I am the Fatal Hammer Blow!
I am the Whistler in the Dark, I am Putrefaction's Fishy Mark!
I am the Three-legged Wheel!
I am the Towering Column of Fire before which the ape masturbates his life entire!

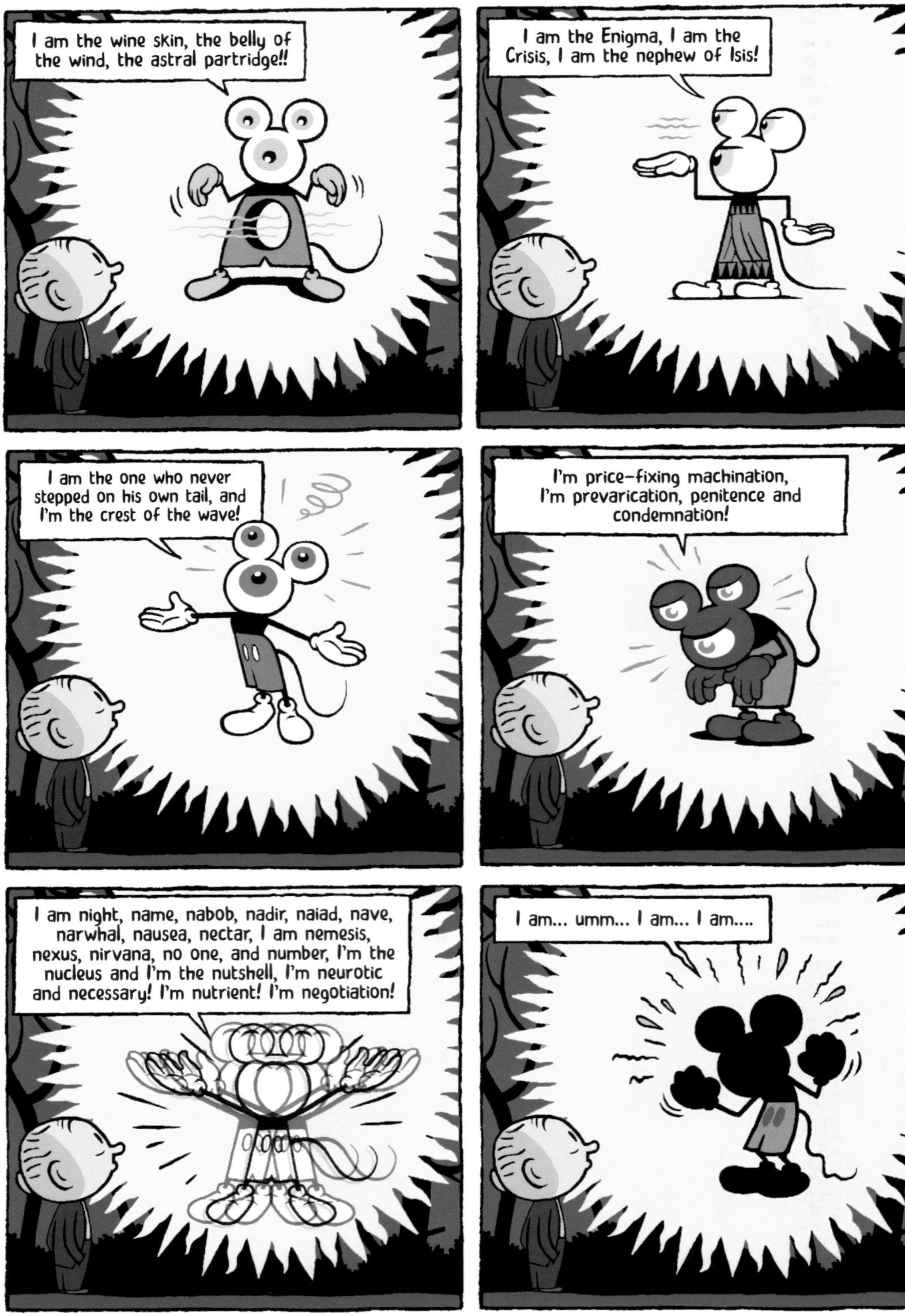
I am the wine skin, the belly of the wind, the astral partridge!!
I am the Enigma, I am the Crisis, I am the nephew of Isis!
I am the one who never stepped on his own tail, and I'm the crest of the wave!
I'm price-fixing machination, I'm prevarication, penitence and condemnation!
I am night, name, nabob, nadir, naiad, nave, narwhal, nausea, nectar, I am nemesis, nexus, nirvana, no one, and number, I'm the nucleus and I'm the nutshell, I'm neurotic and necessary! I'm nutrient! I'm negotiation!
I am... umm... I am... I am....

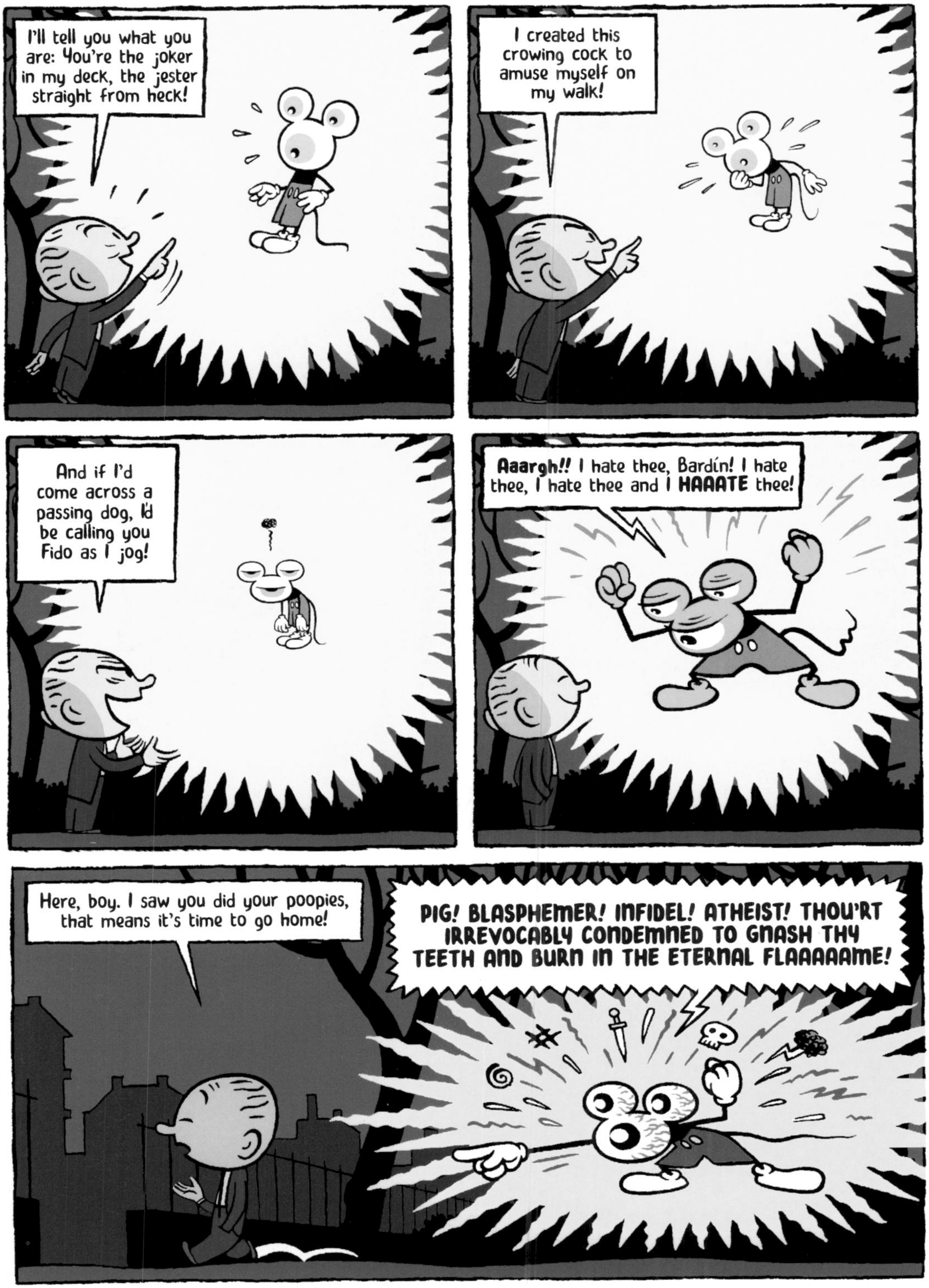
I'll tell you what you are: You're the joker in my deck, the jester straight from heck!
I created this crowing cock to amuse myself on my walk!
And if I'd come across a passing dog, I'd be calling you Fido as I jog!
Aaargh!! I hate thee, Bardín! I hate thee, I hate thee and I HAAATE thee!
Here, boy. I saw you did your poopies, that means it's time to go home!
PIG! BLASPHEMER! INFIDEL! ATHEIST! THOU'RT IRREVOCABLY CONDEMNED TO GNASH THY TEETH AND BURN IN THE ETERNAL FLAAAAAME!

in the park

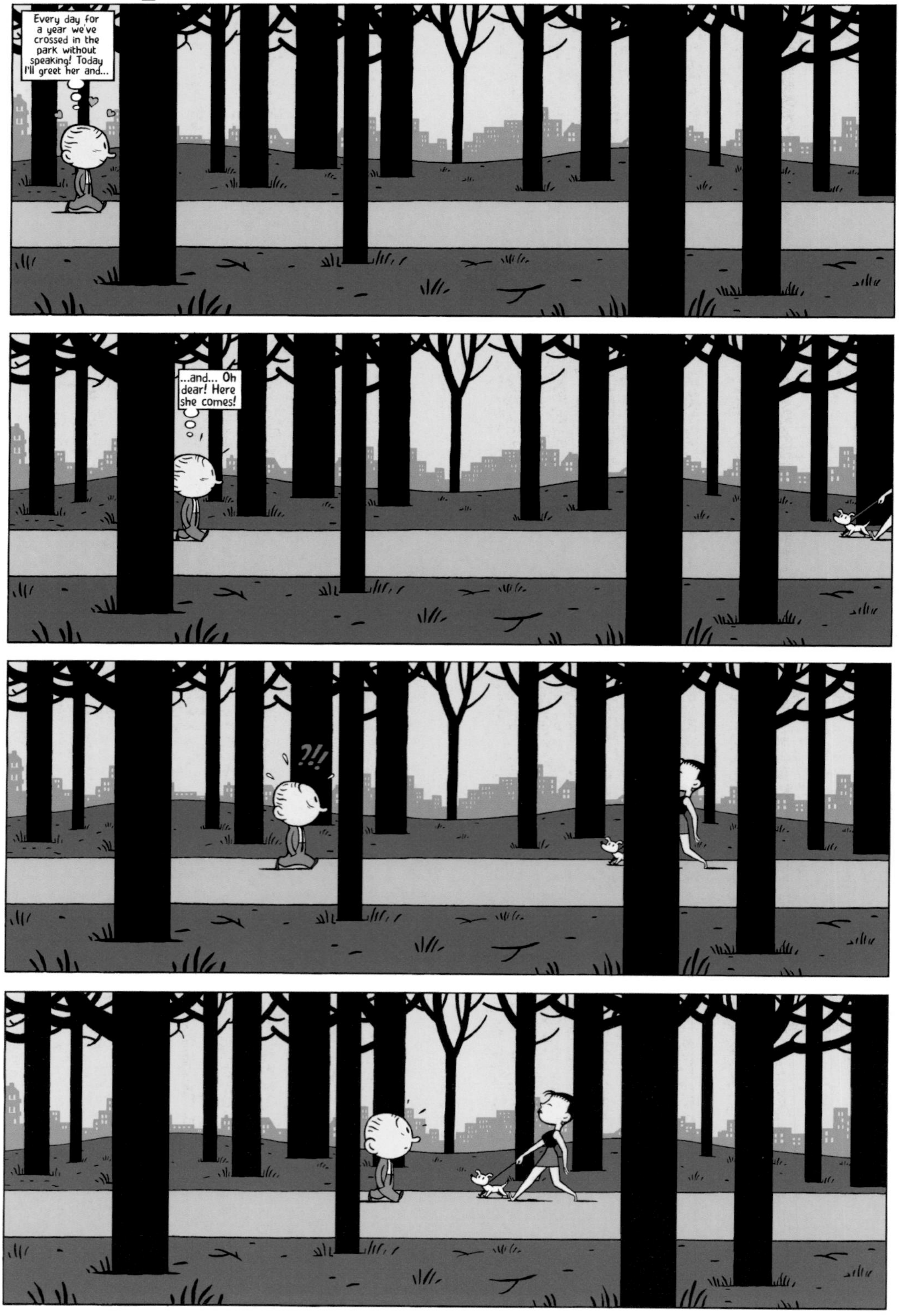

Every day for a year we've crossed in the park without speaking! Today I'll greet her and...
...and... Oh dear! Here she comes!
?!!

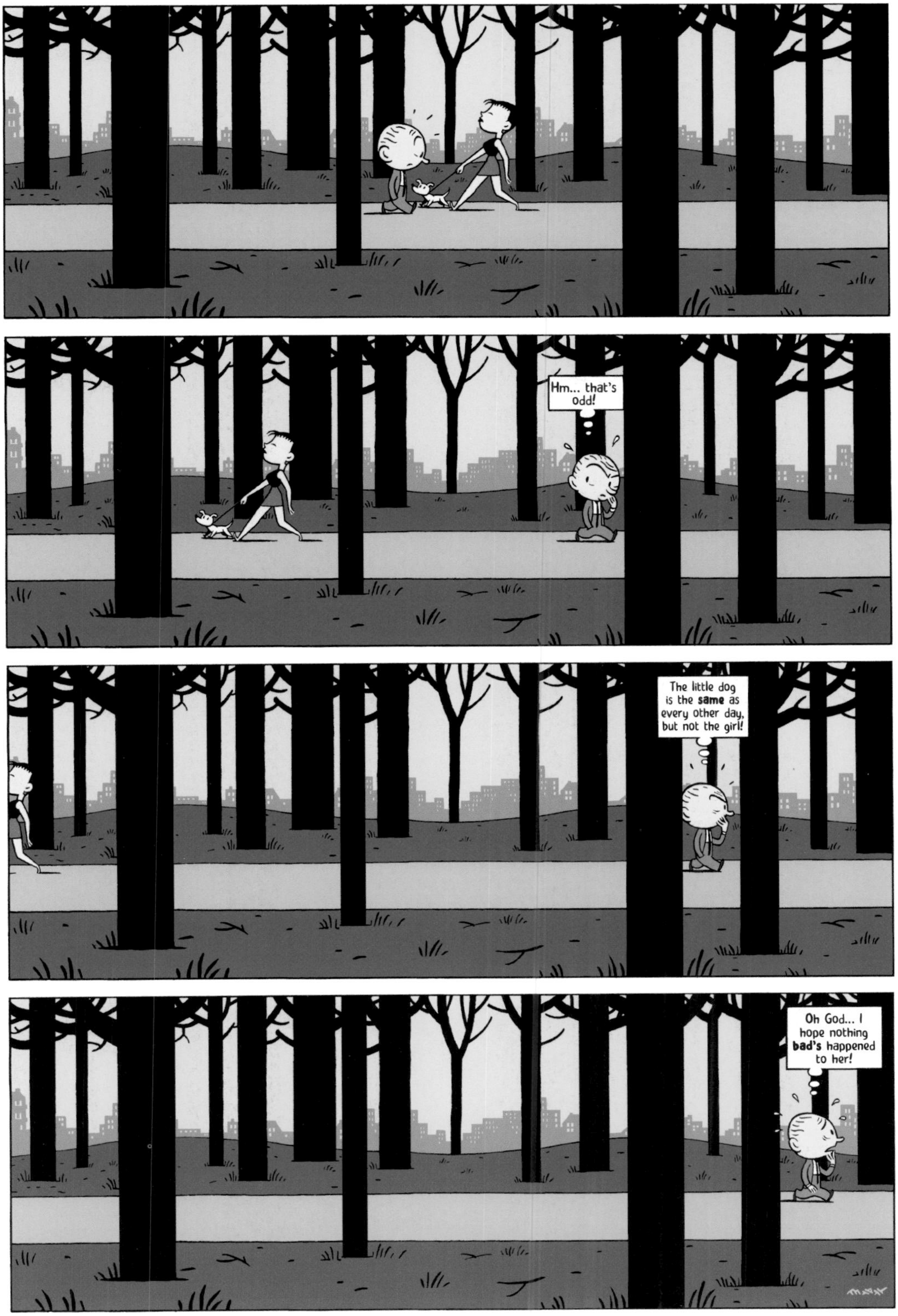

Hm... that's odd!
The little dog is the **same** as every other day, but not the girl!
Oh God... I hope nothing **bad's** happened to her!

Bardín's description of the superreal world.

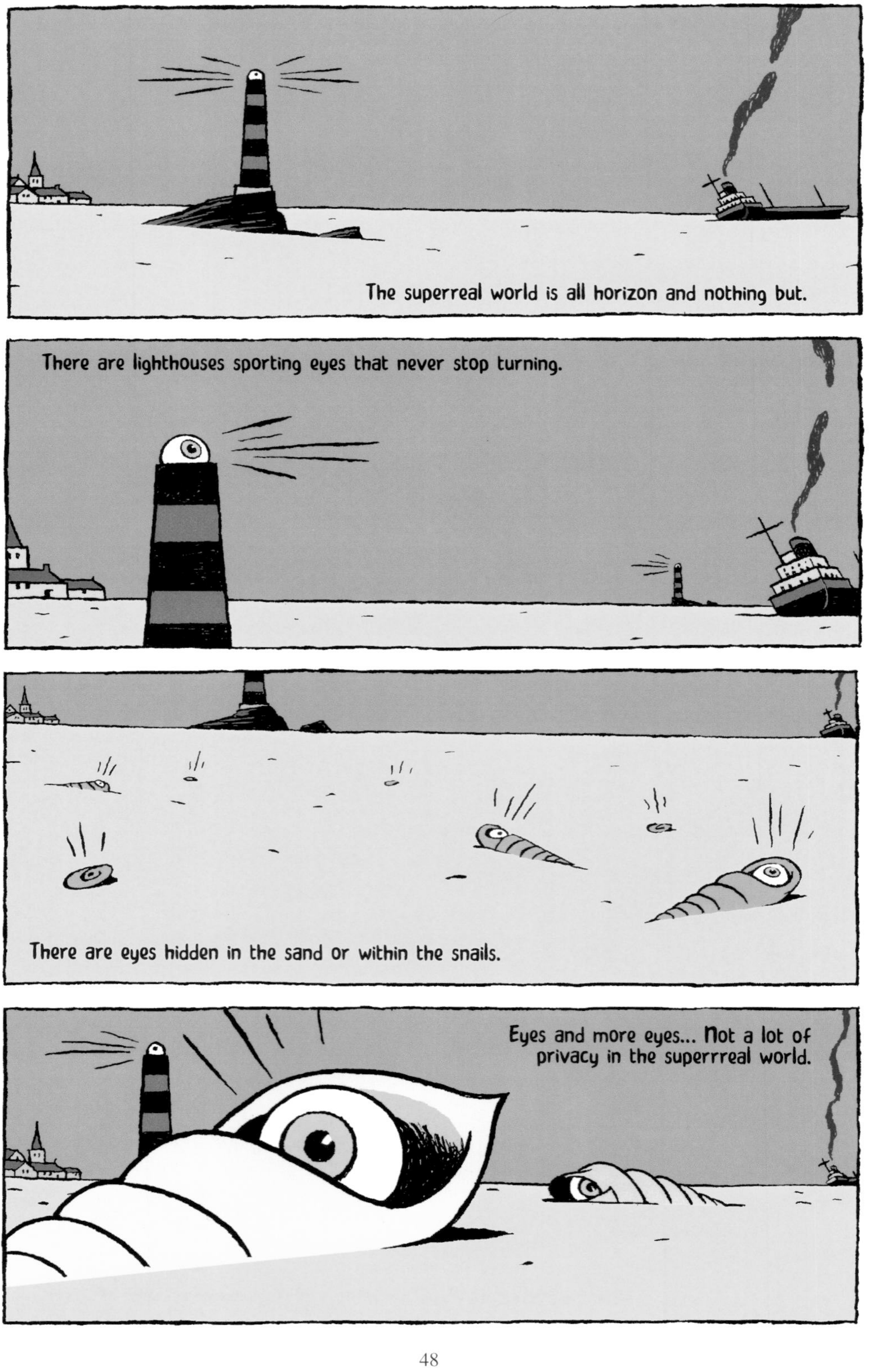
The superreal world is all horizon and nothing but.
There are lighthouses sporting eyes that never stop turning.
There are eyes hidden in the sand or within the snails.
Eyes and more eyes... Not a lot of privacy in the superrreal world.

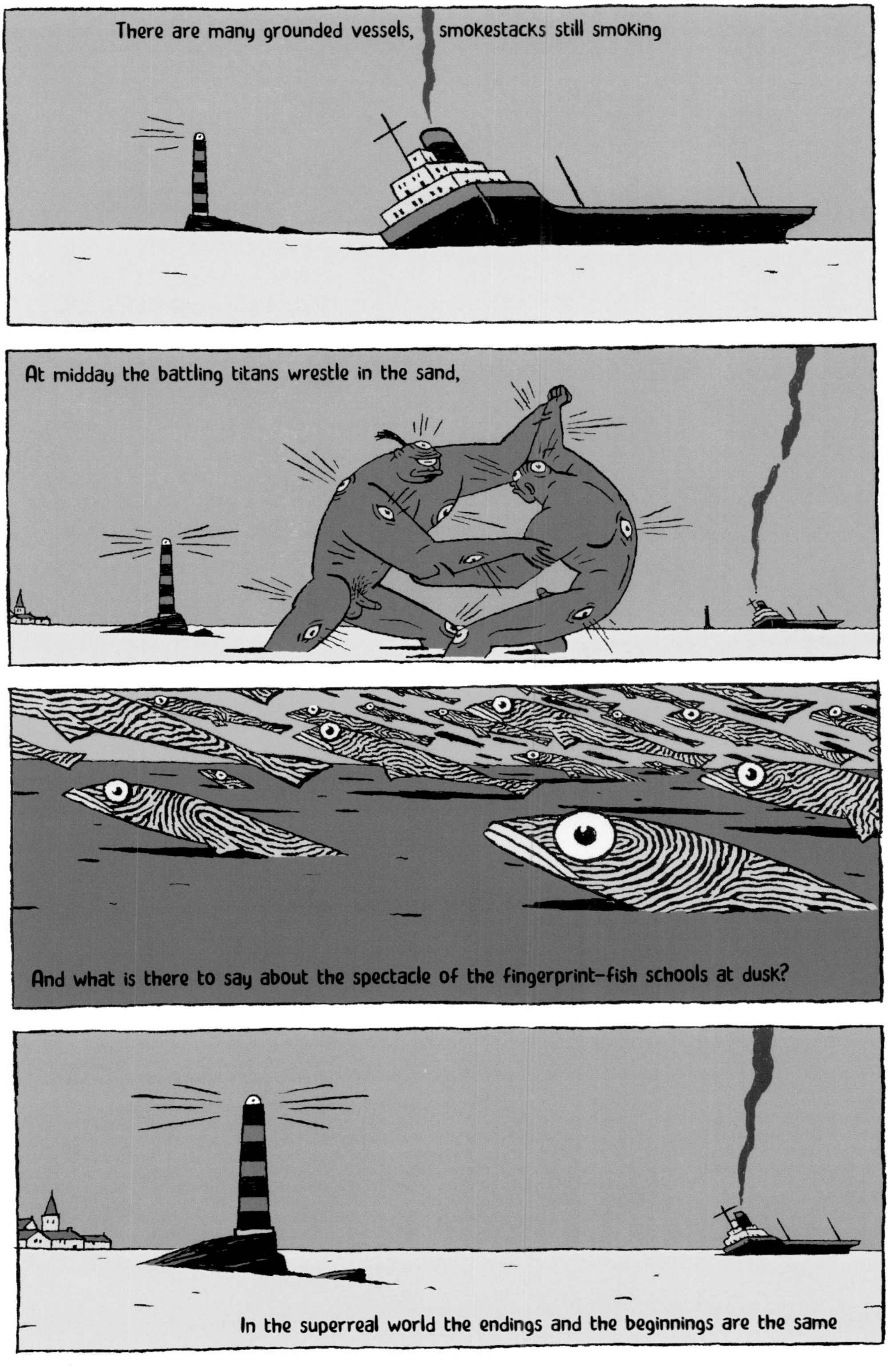
There are many grounded vessels, smokestacks still smoking
At midday the battling titans wrestle in the sand,
And what is there to say about the spectacle of the fingerprint-fish schools at dusk?
In the superreal world the endings and the beginnings are the same

the intricate and tormented conscience of Bardín

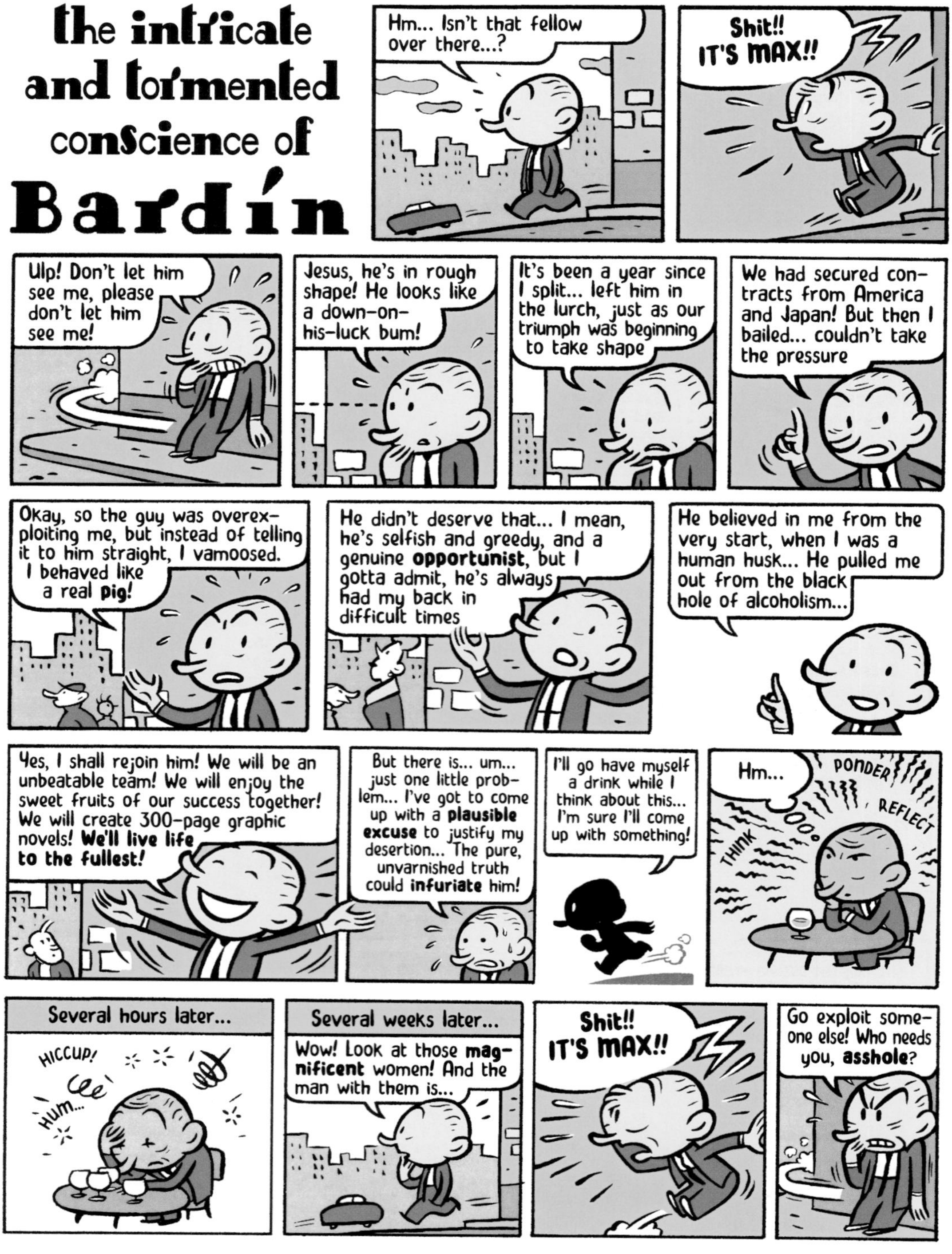

Hm... Isn't that fellow over there...?
Shit!! IT'S MAX!!
Ulp! Don't let him see me, please don't let him see me!
Jesus, he's in rough shape! He looks like a down-on-his-luck bum!
It's been a year since I split... left him in the lurch, just as our triumph was beginning to take shape
We had secured contracts from America and Japan! But then I bailed... couldn't take the pressure
Okay, so the guy was overexploiting me, but instead of telling it to him straight, I vamoosed. I behaved like a real pig!
He didn't deserve that... I mean, he's selfish and greedy, and a genuine opportunist, but I gotta admit, he's always had my back in difficult times
He believed in me from the very start, when I was a human husk... He pulled me out from the black hole of alcoholism...
Yes, I shall rejoin him! We will be an unbeatable team! We will enjoy the sweet fruits of our success together! We will create 300-page graphic novels! We'll live life to the fullest!
But there is... um... just one little problem... I've got to come up with a plausible excuse to justify my desertion... The pure, unvarnished truth could infuriate him!
I'll go have myself a drink while I think about this... I'm sure I'll come up with something!
Hm...
PONDER
REFLECT
THINK
Several hours later...
HICCUP!
HUM...
Several weeks later...
Wow! Look at those magnificent women! And the man with them is...
Shit!! IT'S MAX!!
Go exploit someone else! Who needs you, asshole?

BARDÍN the Superrealist 3/11/04

Gee, Cirlot, isn't it a bit early in the day to be heading out for cognacs?
You're right, Bardín. Why don't we go check out the guy who climbed up the smokestack of the old tile factory instead?
Oh, right, the one who thinks he's Simon of the Desert! They say he's some-thing to behold!
Indeed, the guy delivers these incredibly mystical perorations, he preaches against the moral corruptions of society, and issues prophecies and portentous revelations
AR
PA
I've heard say he barely eats, and there are those who swear they've seen him levitate... He's got dozens of followers and there are tales of miraculous healings!
Wow, this sounds promising!
There's the lot where he lives!
If you're coming to see Simon, don't waste your time. The guy never says a word
Why is that?
The day the bombs exploded in Madrid he fell silent. He said, "Speaking inanities costs lives." And ever since then he hasn't opened his mouth again!
Geez... That guy clammed up just as he was starting to make sense...

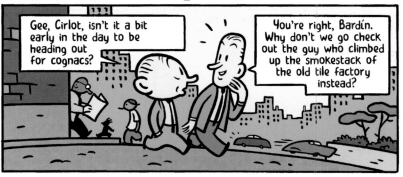

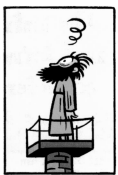

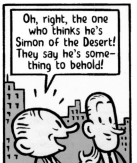

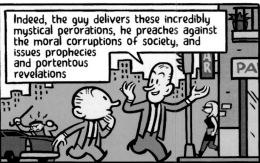

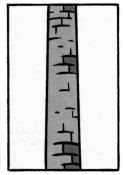

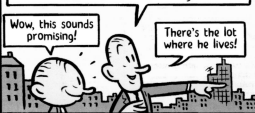

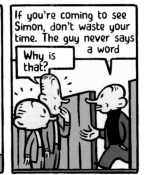

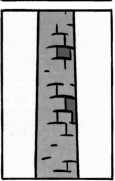

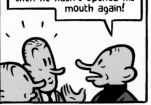

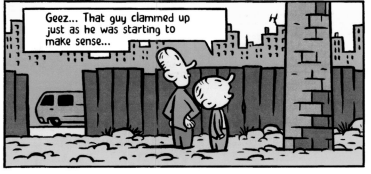

Bardín
the
Superrealist
in
"dimestore
buddha"
What a bargain!!
TODO A 0'99€
There!
The perfect spot!
I'll never tire of contemplating it!
Mmm...
Z
ZZZZ
Happy New Year, Bardín!

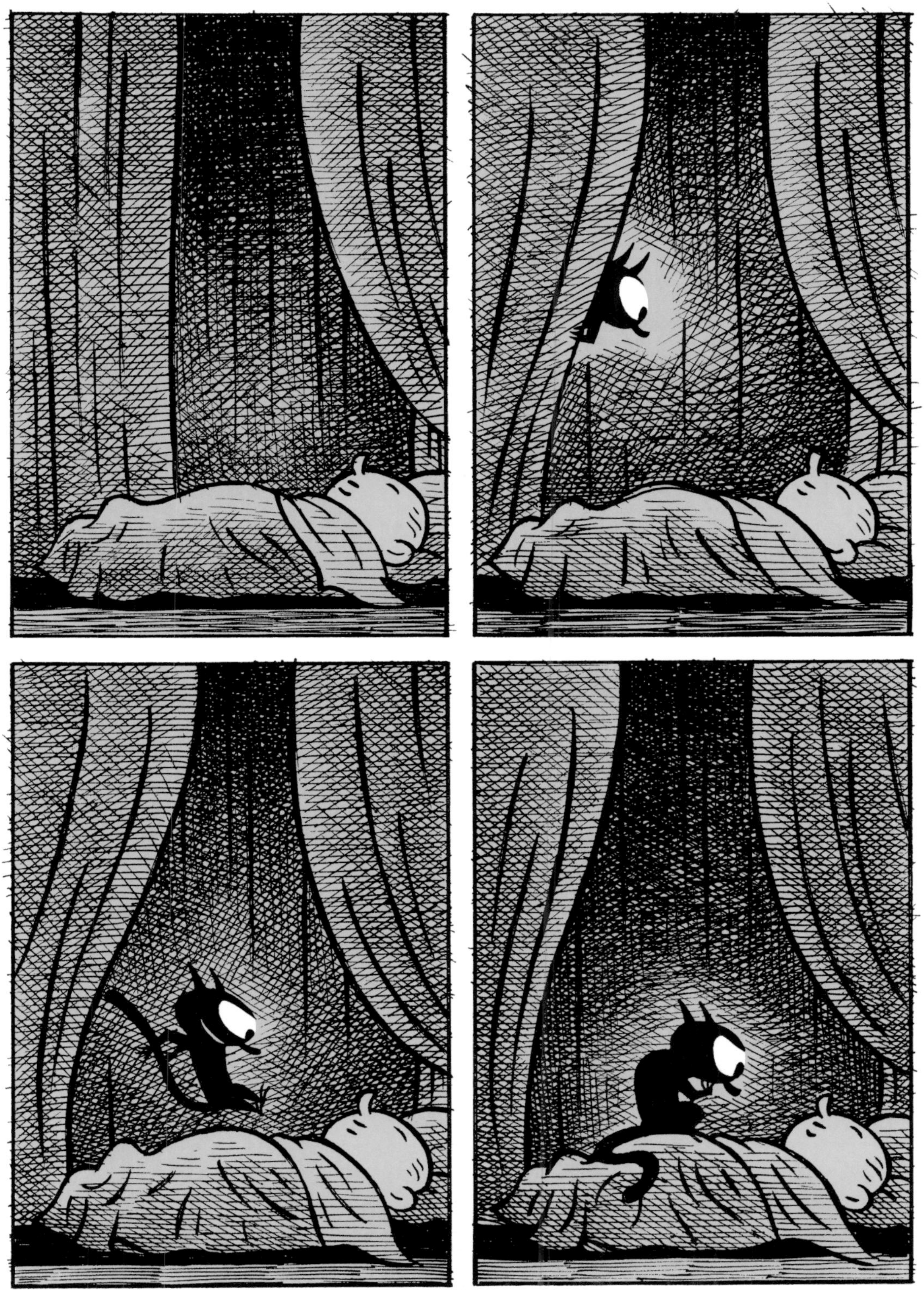

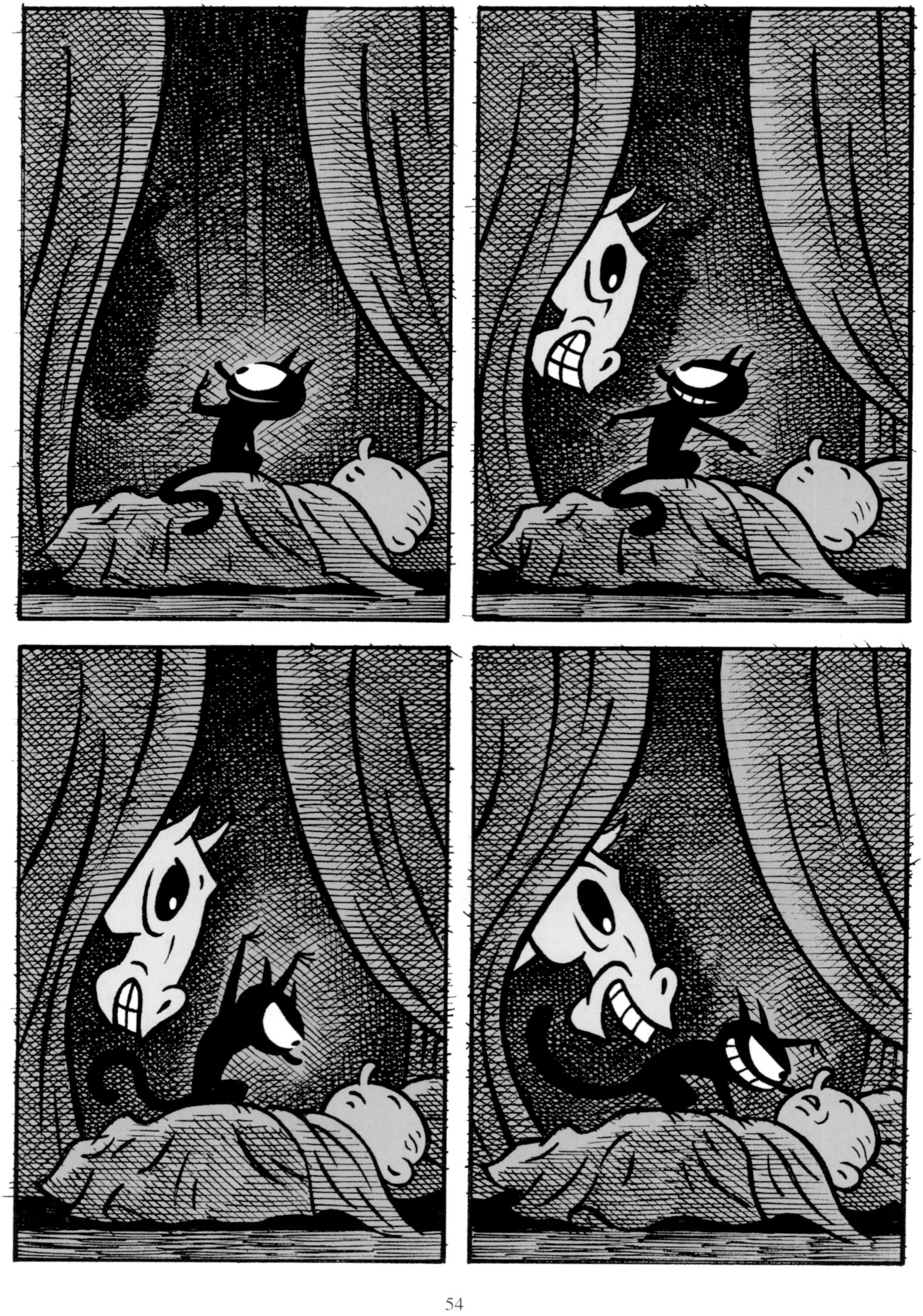

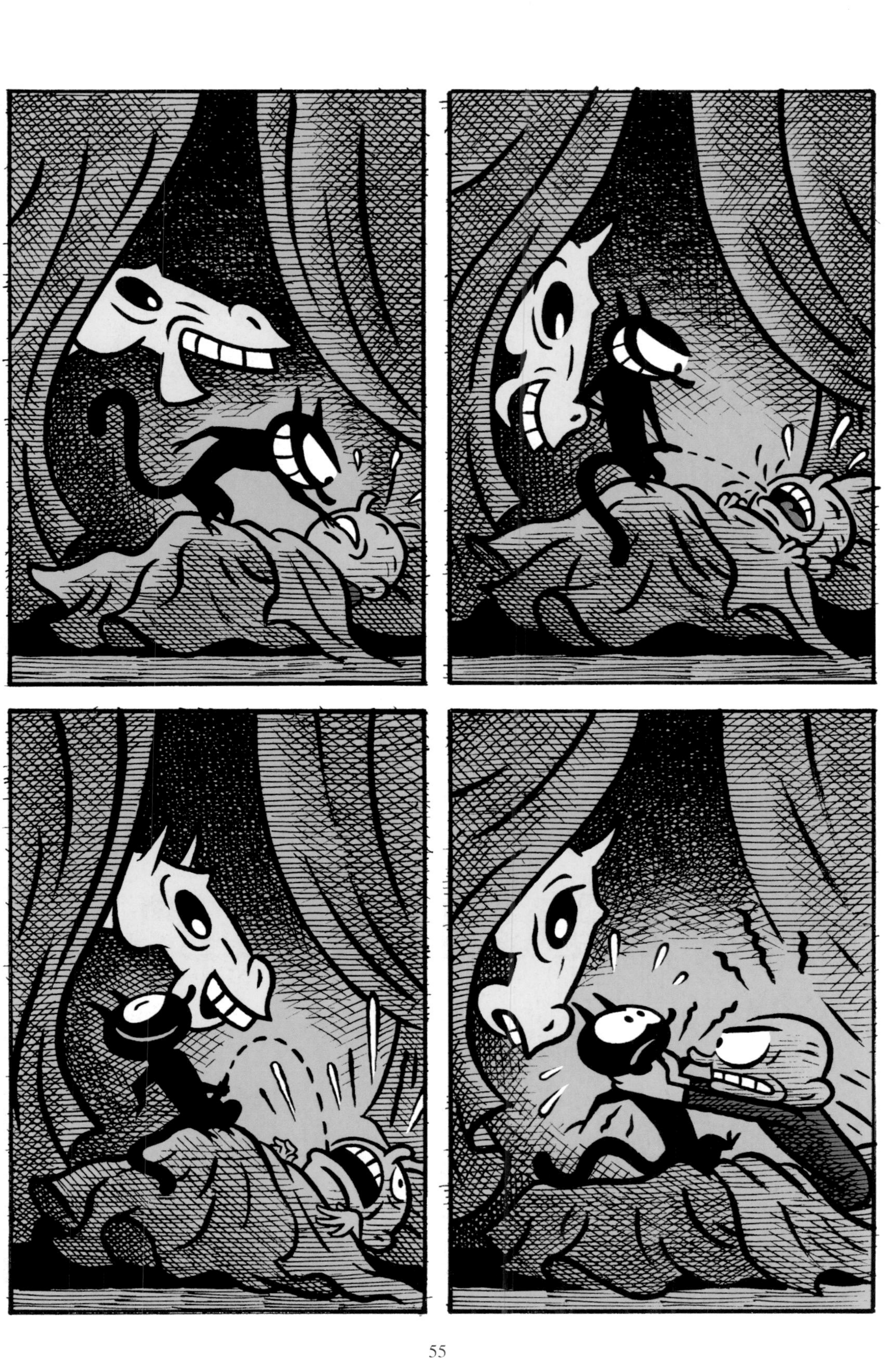

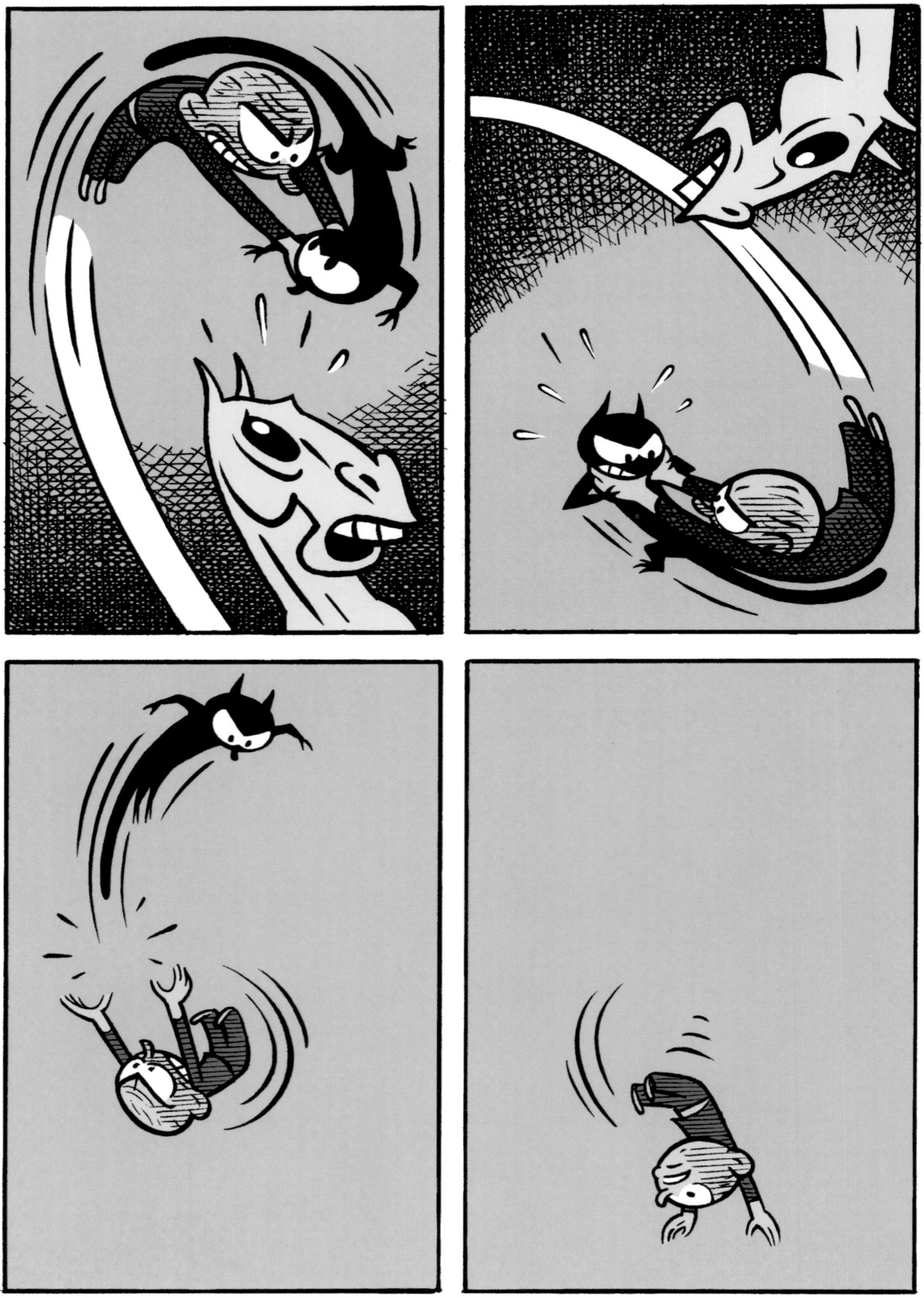

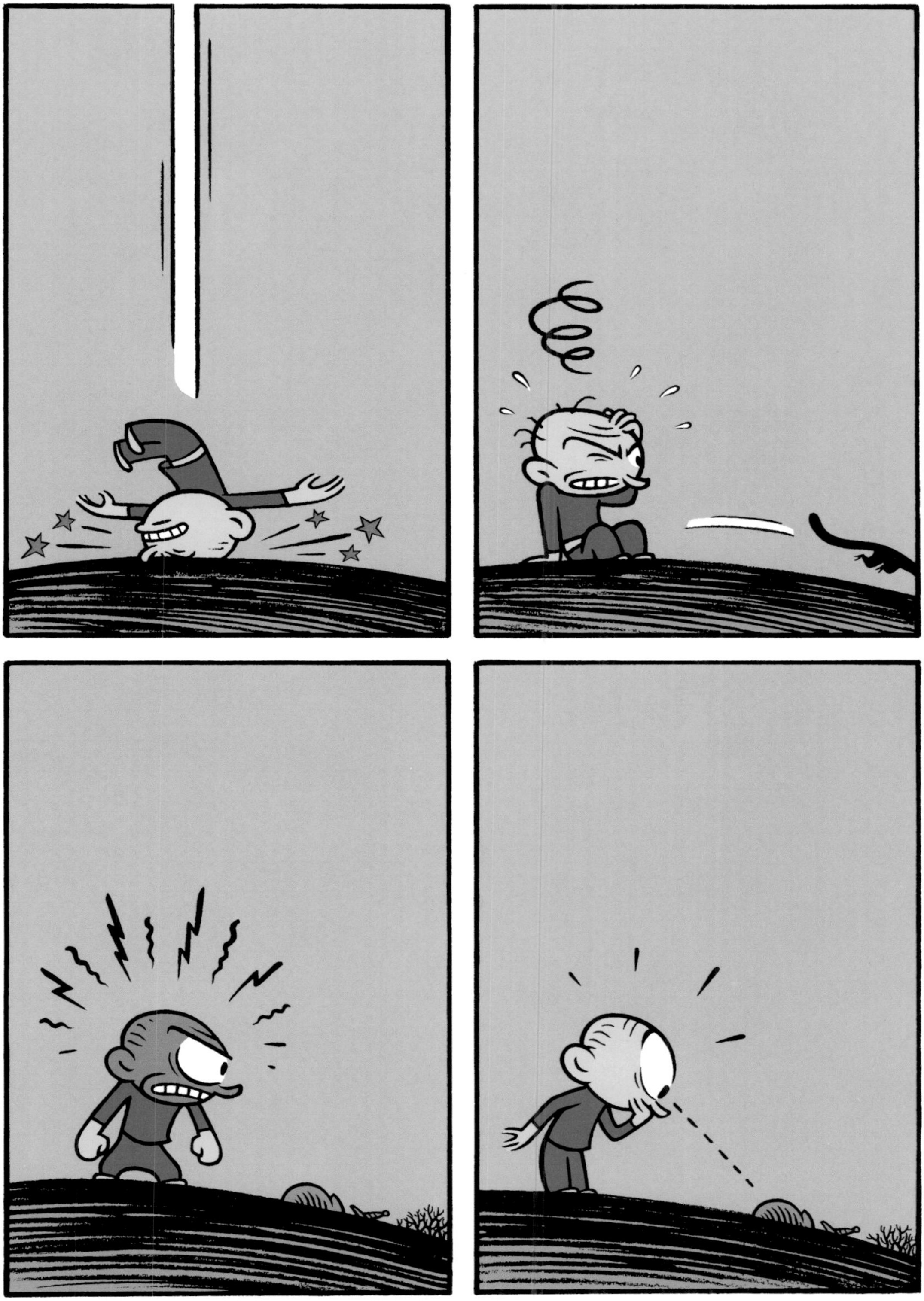

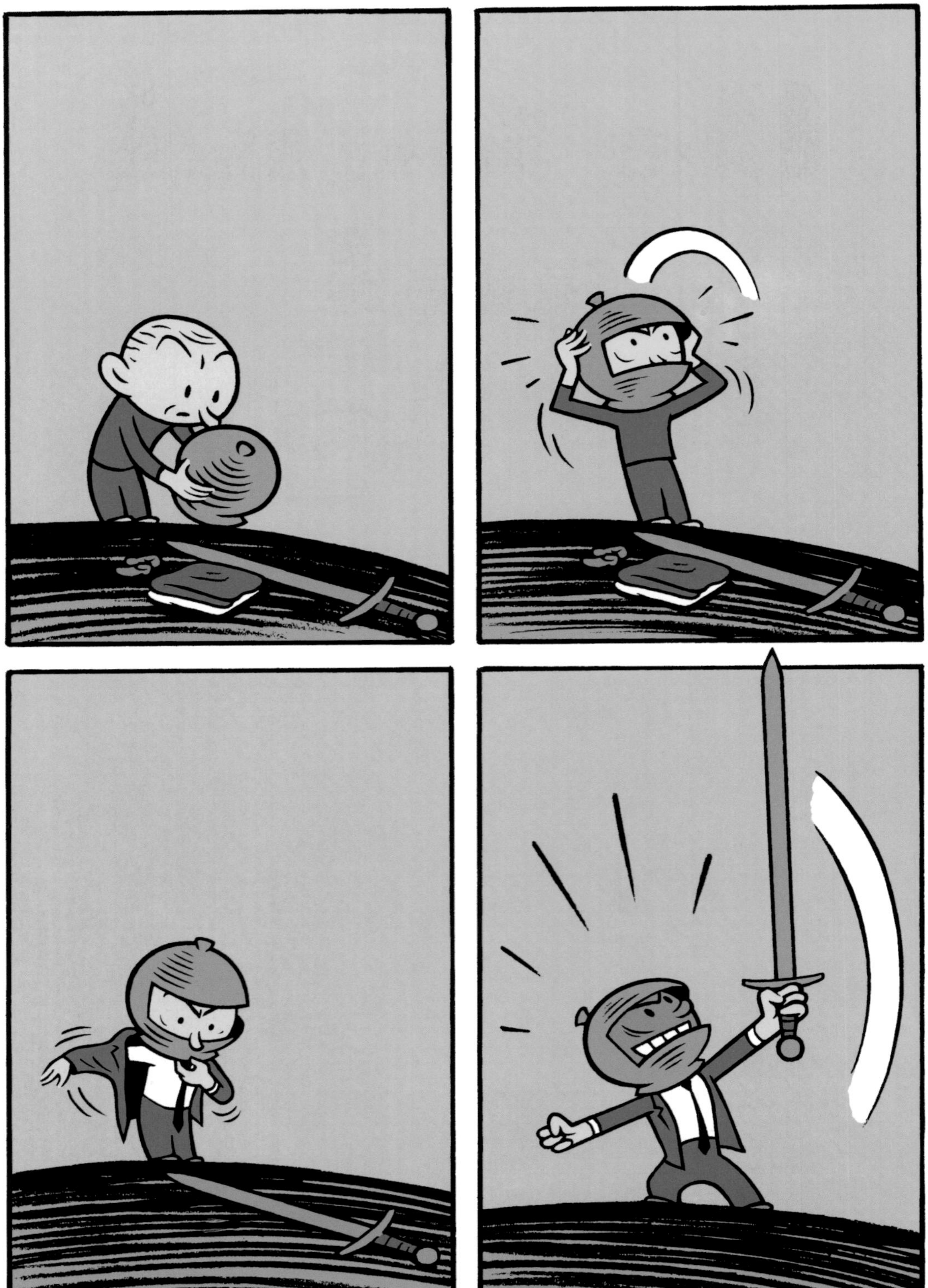

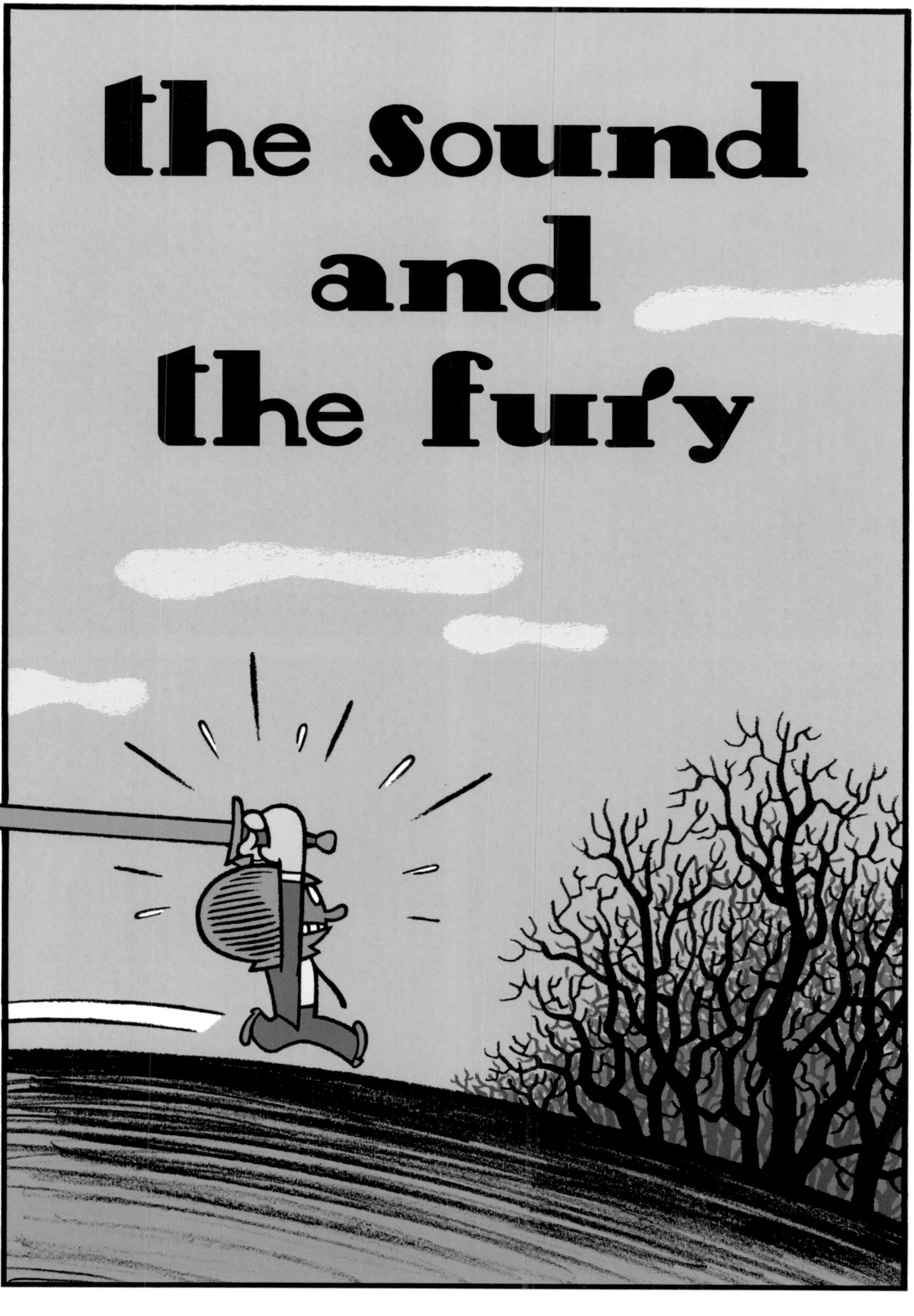
the Sound
and
the fury

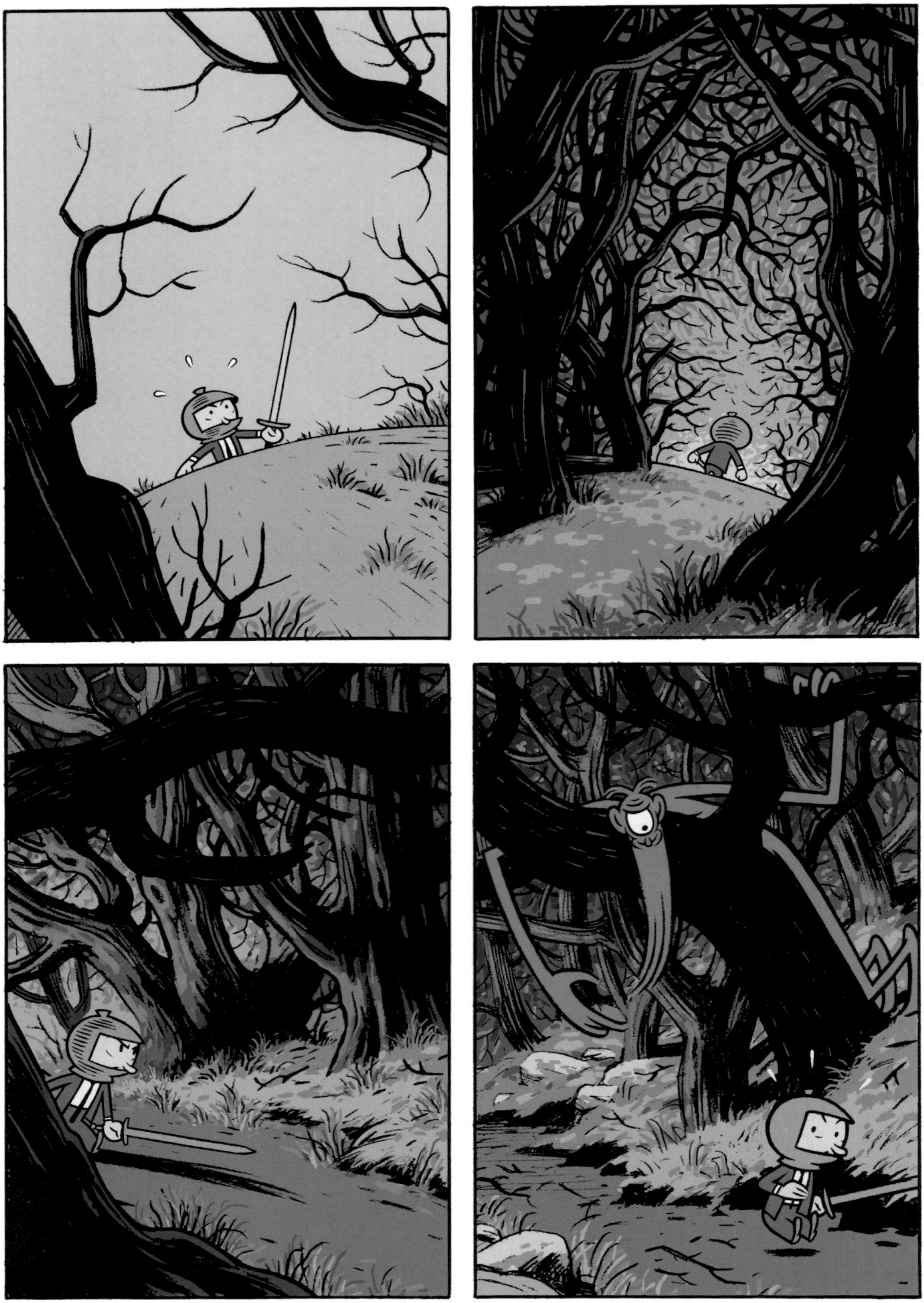

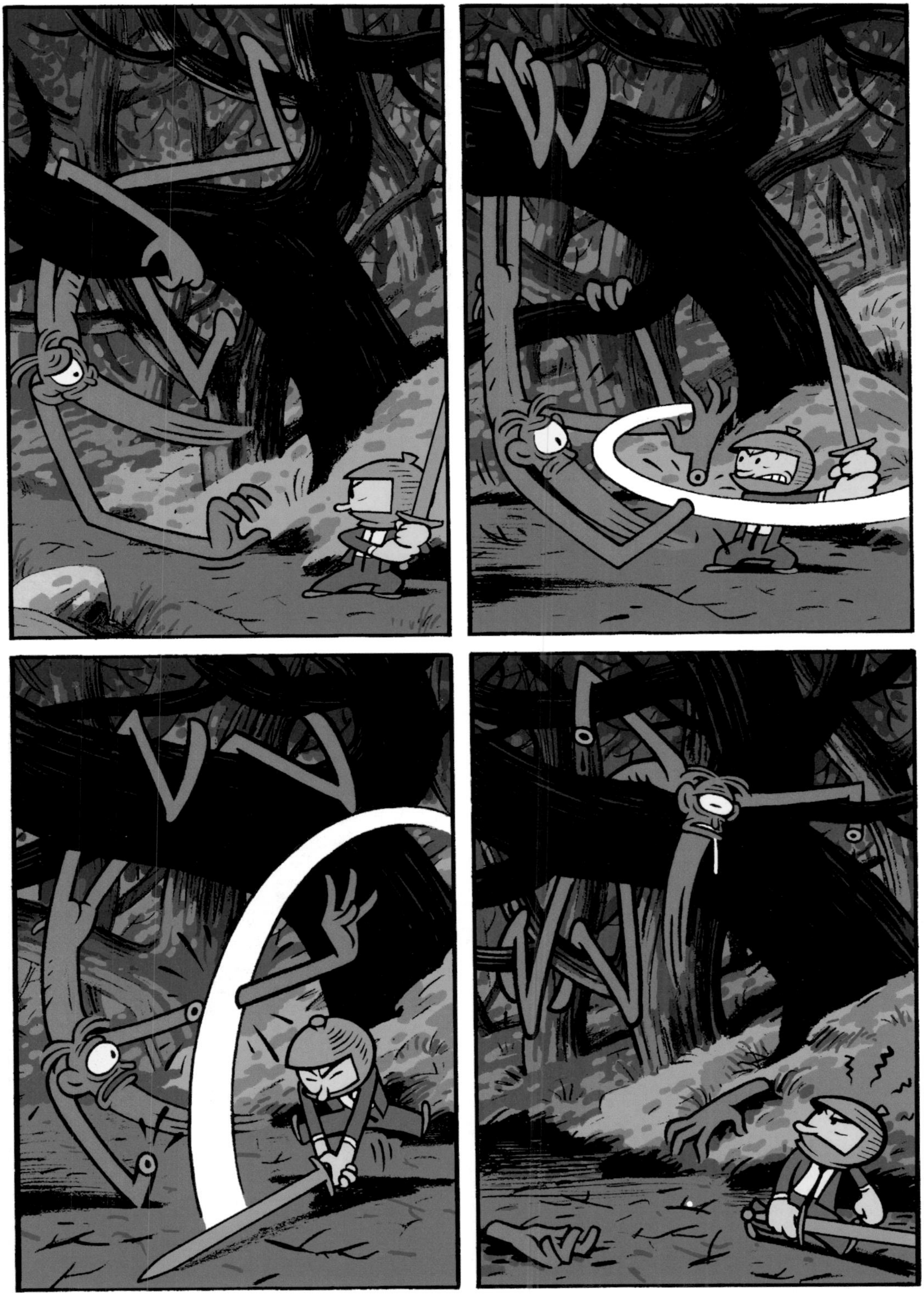

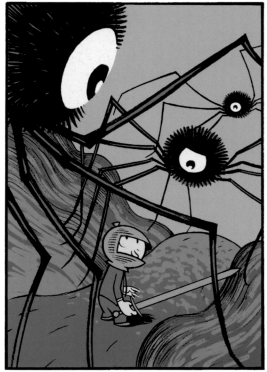

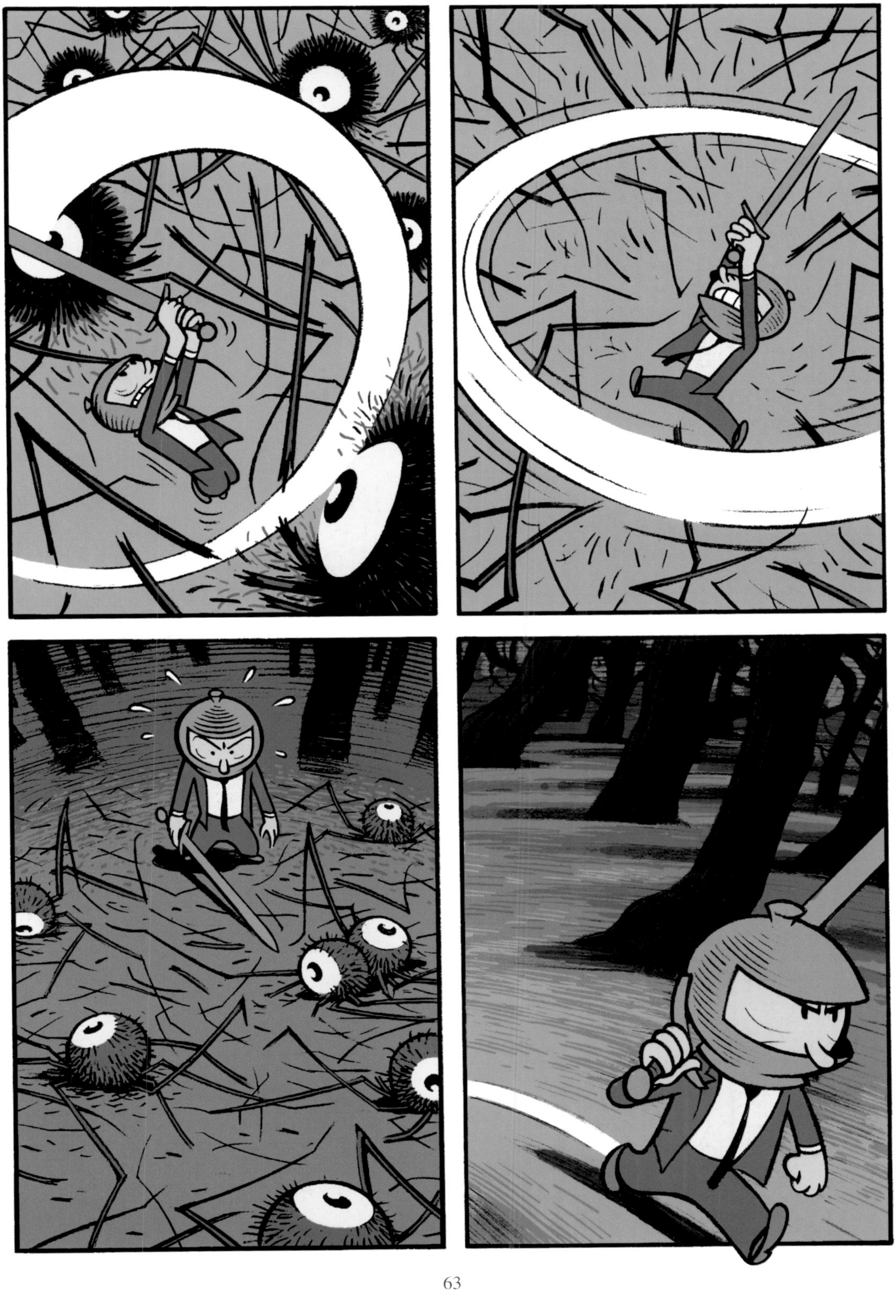

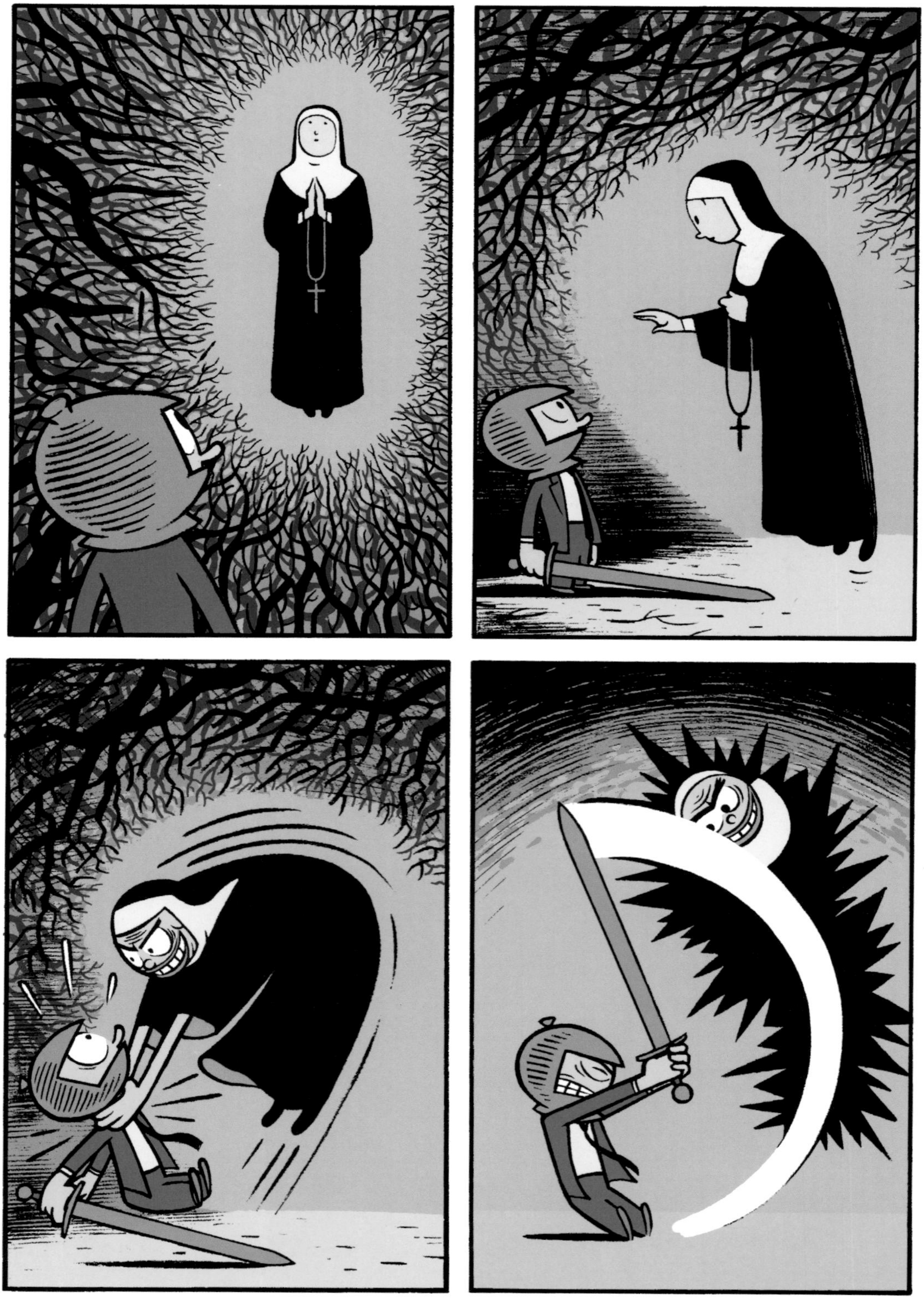

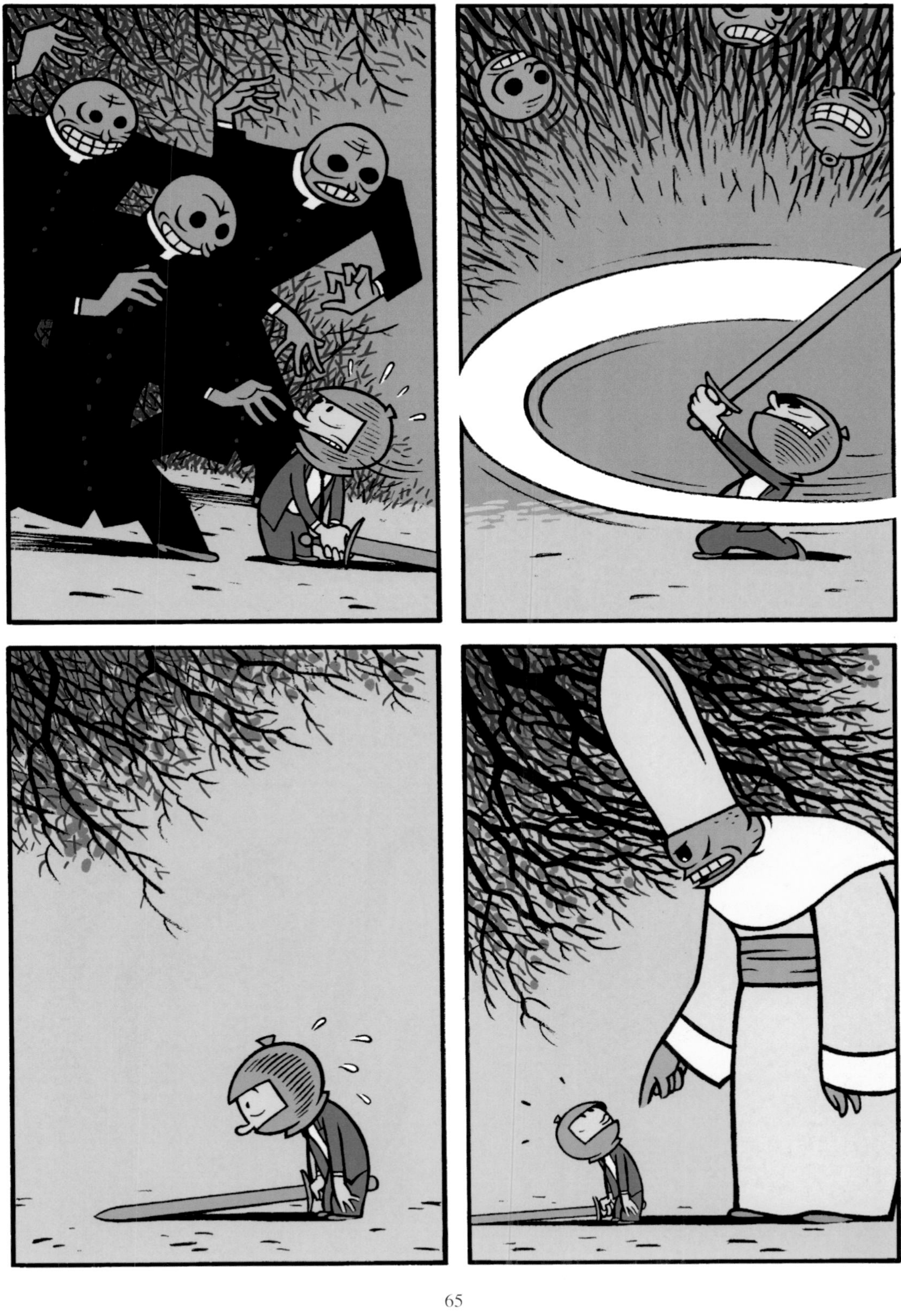

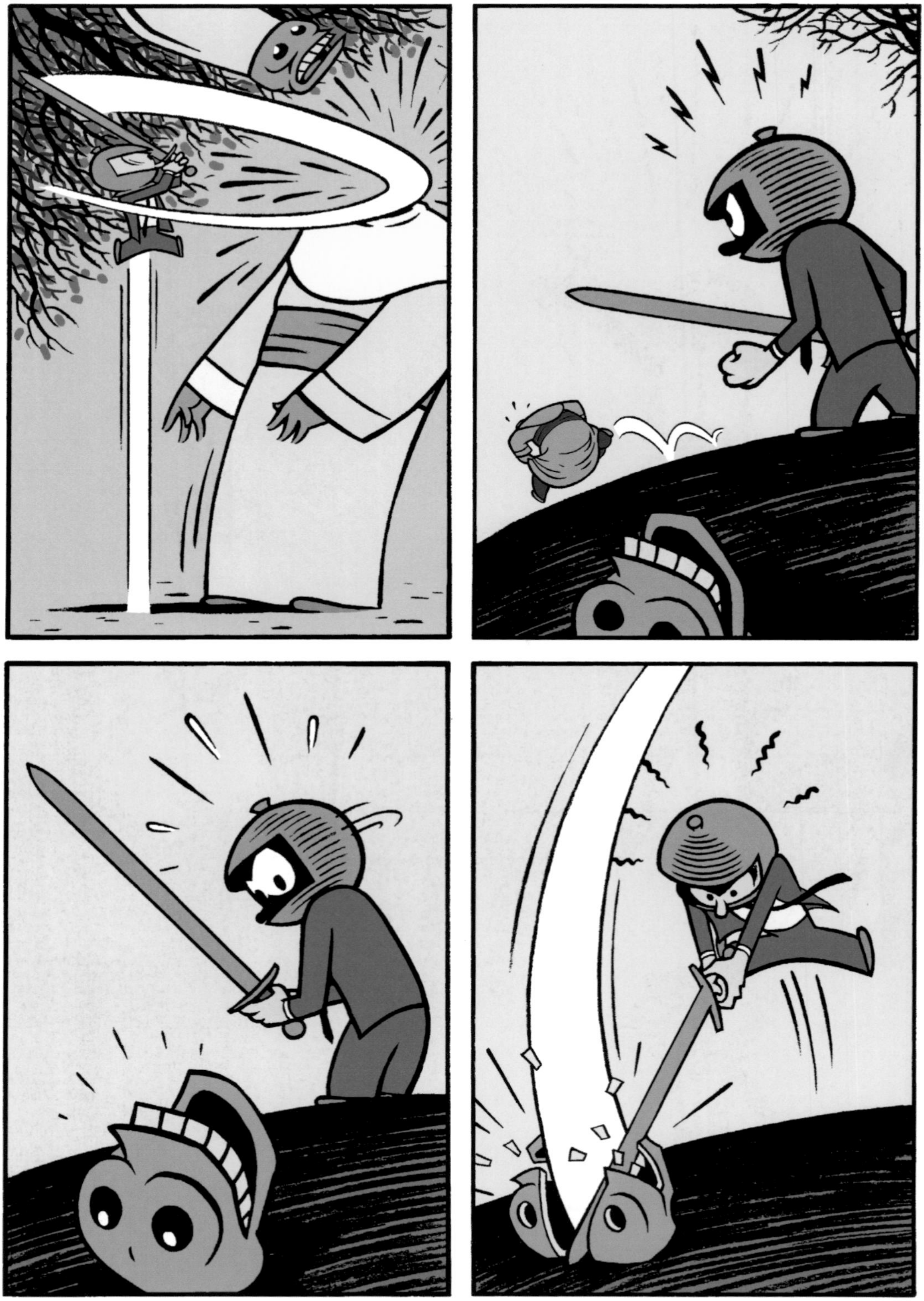

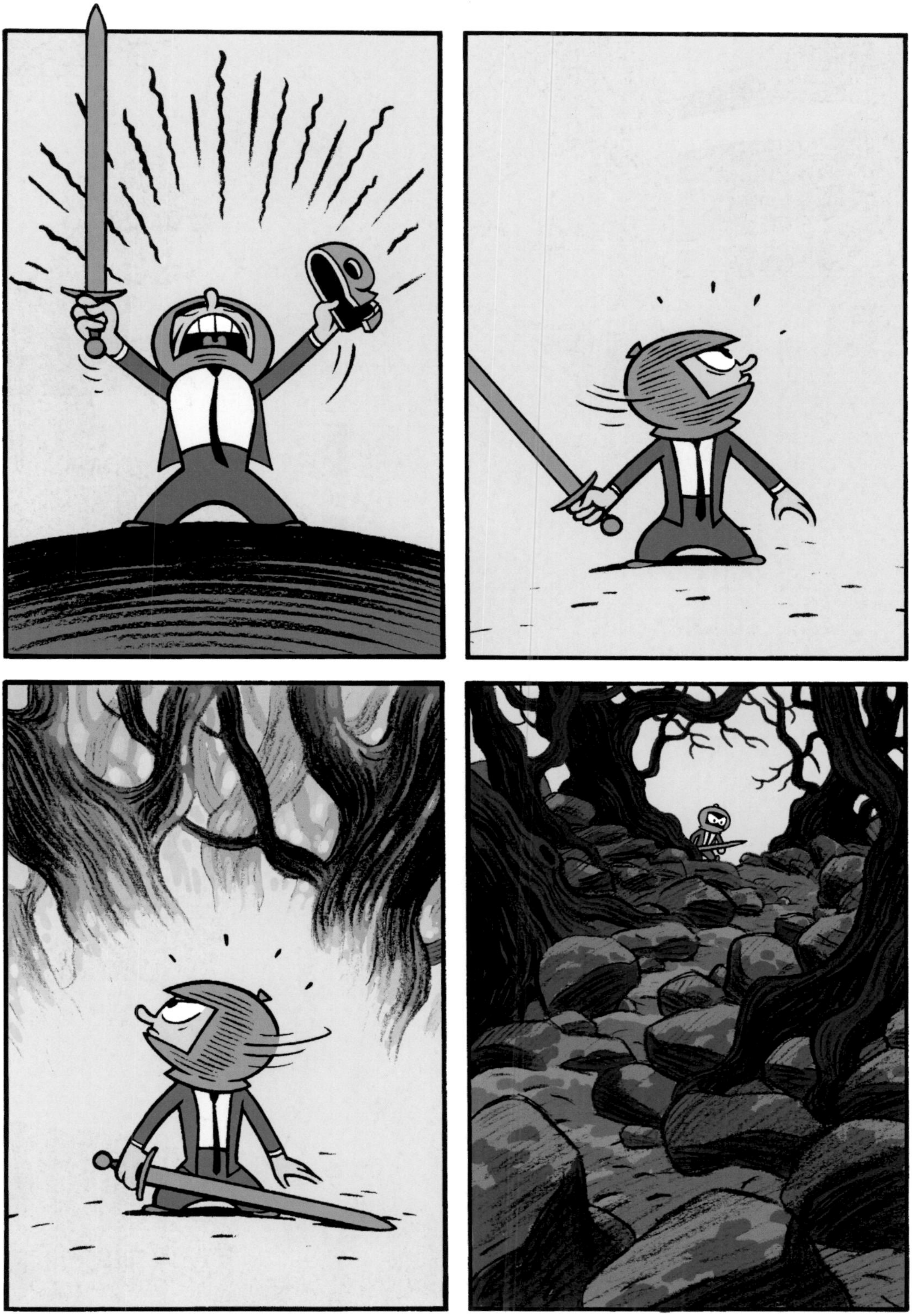

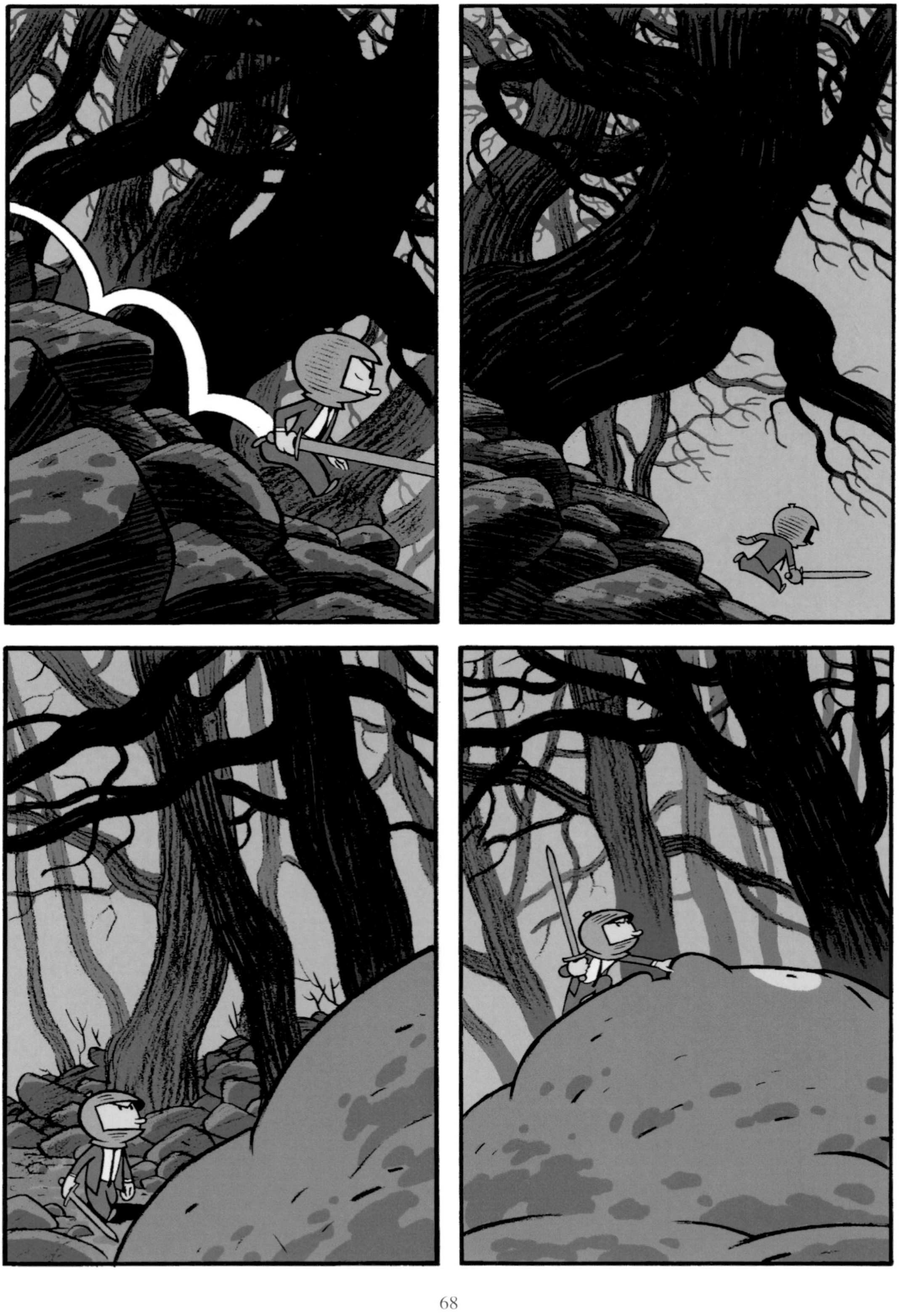

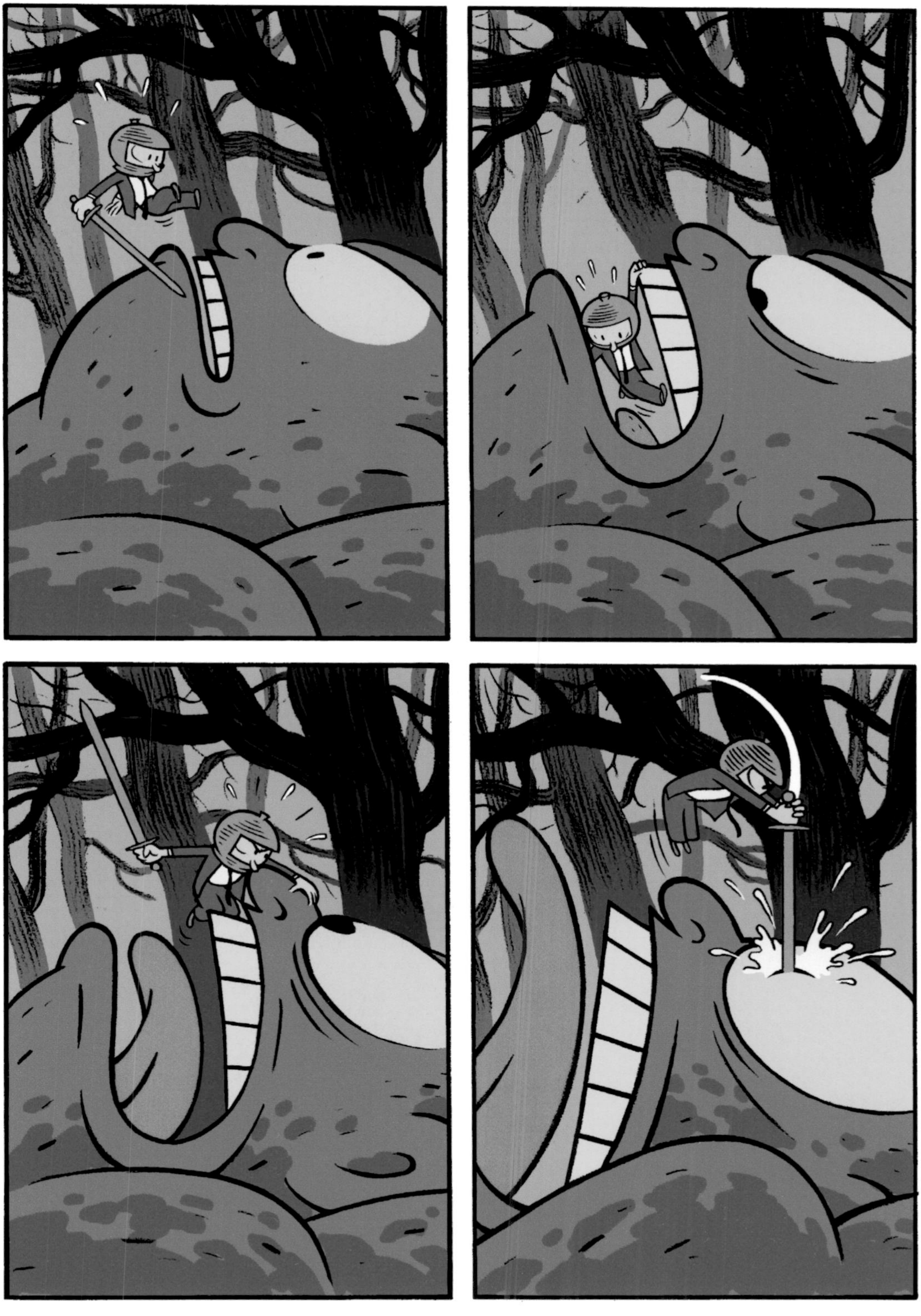

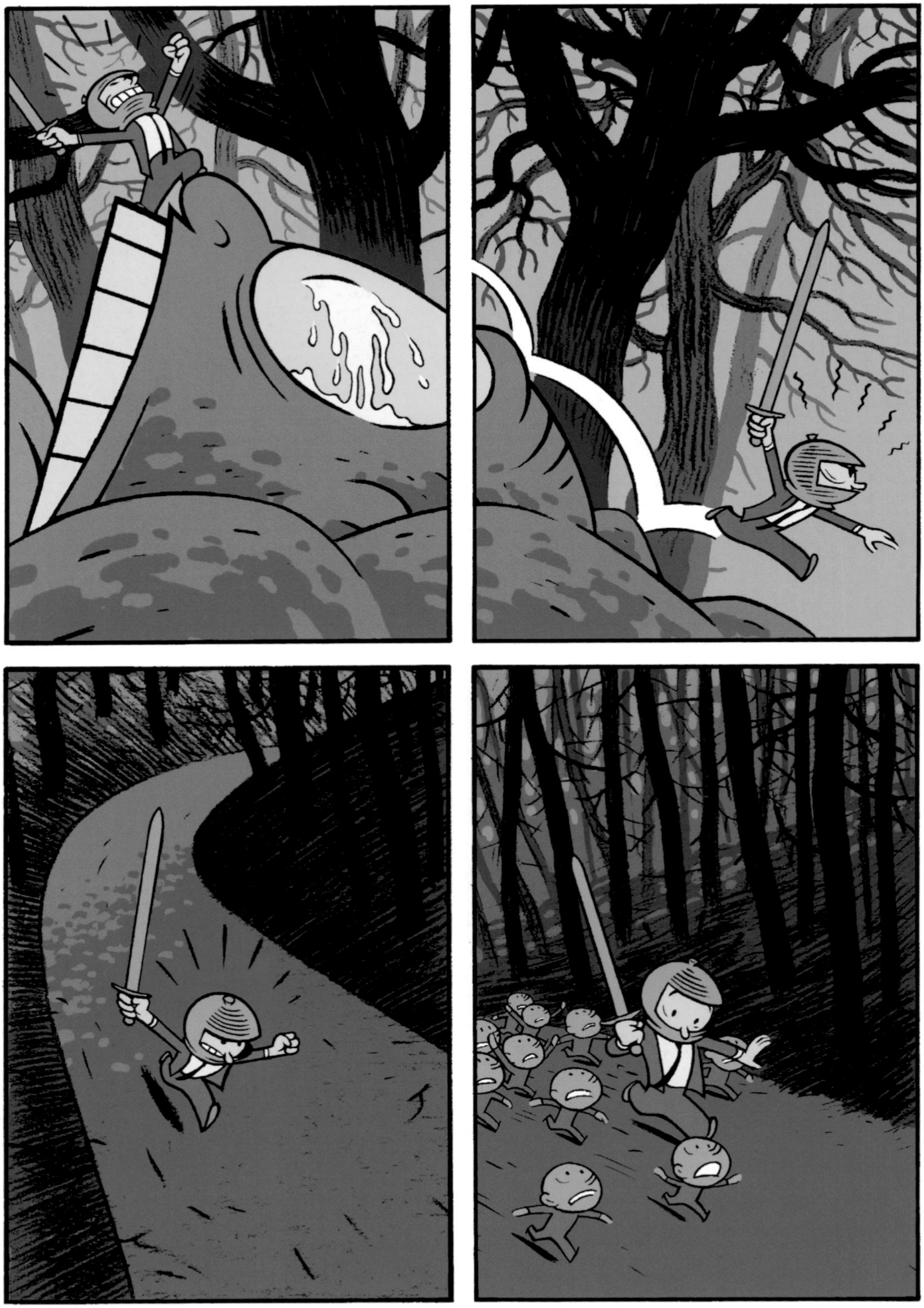

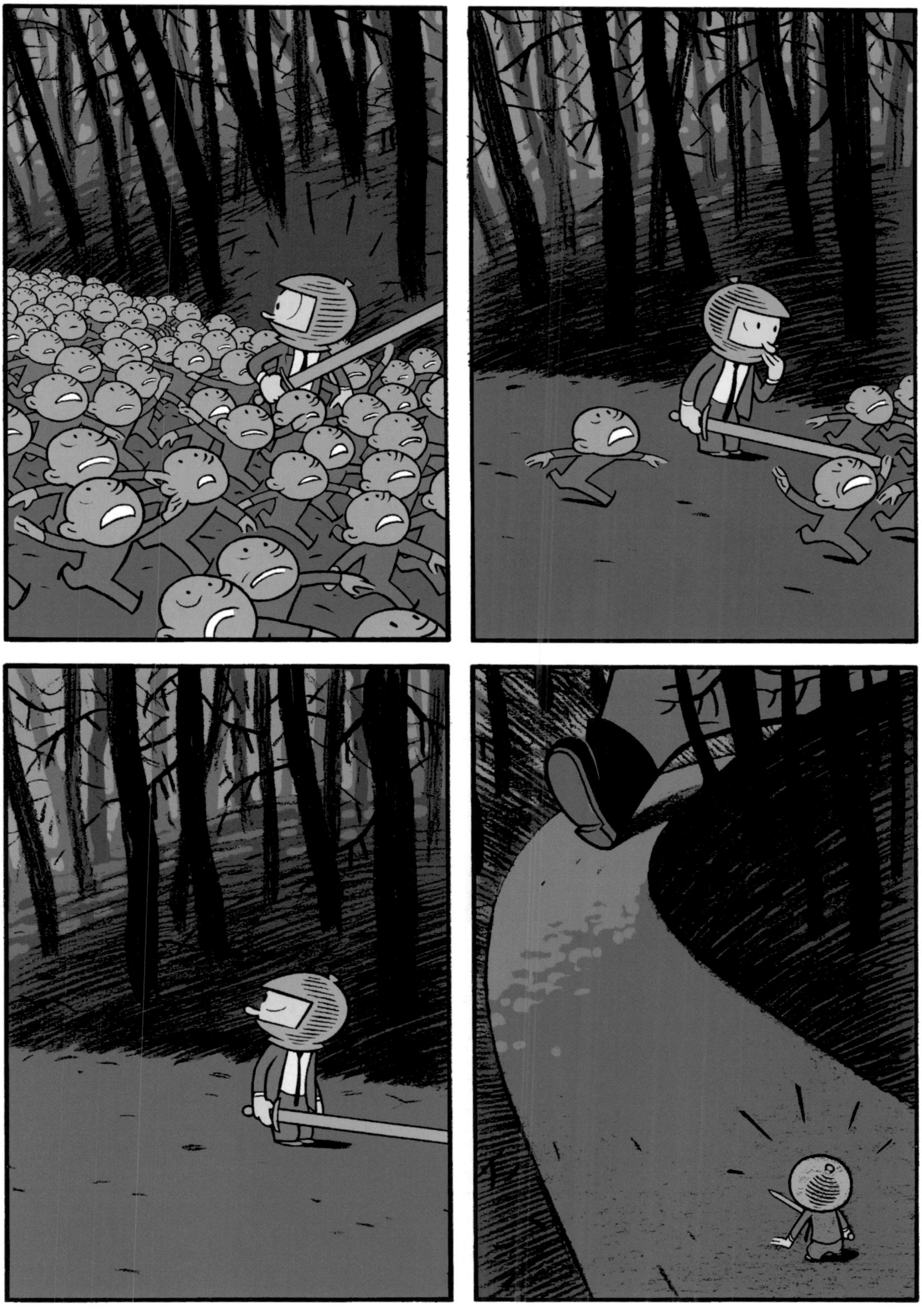

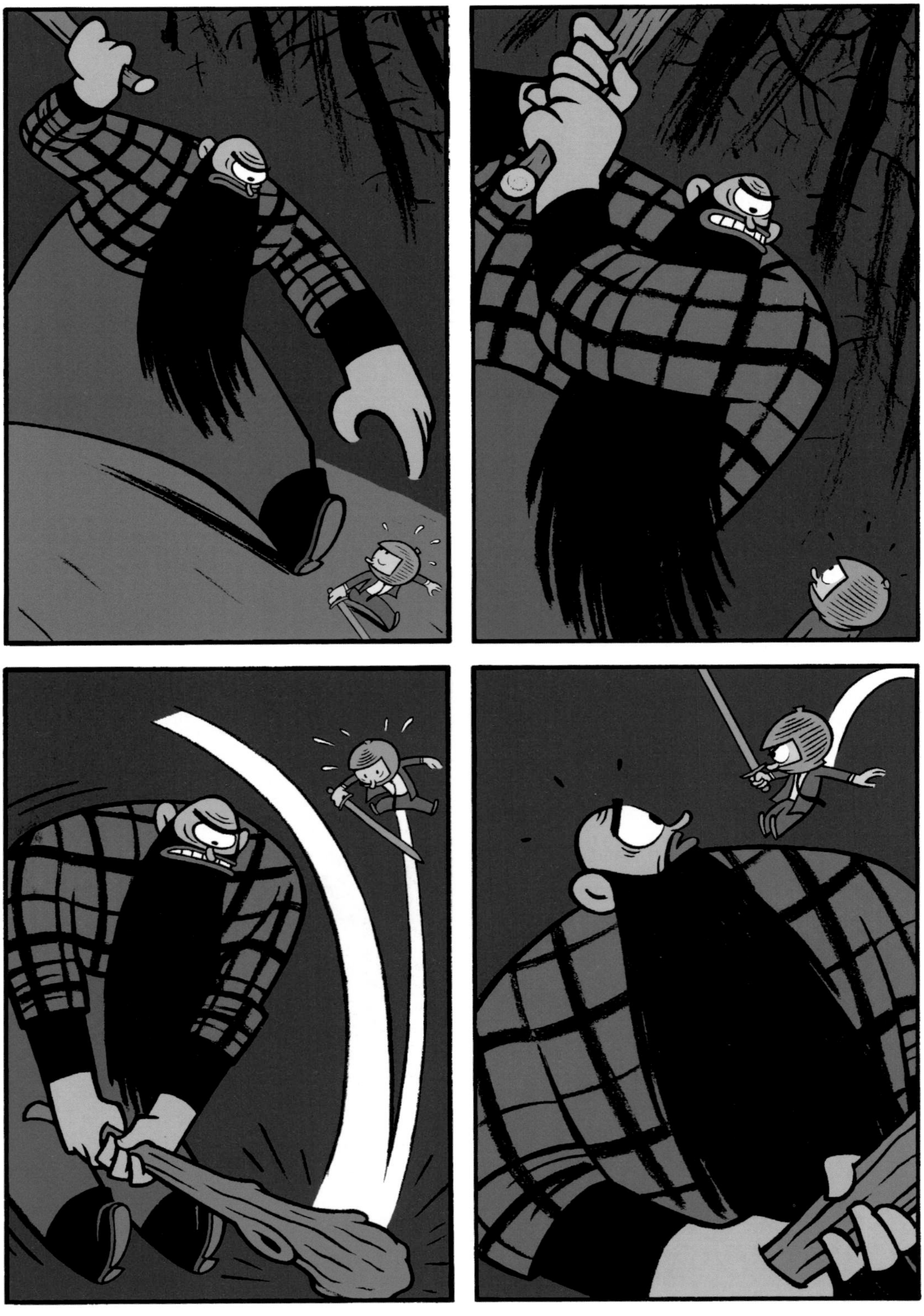

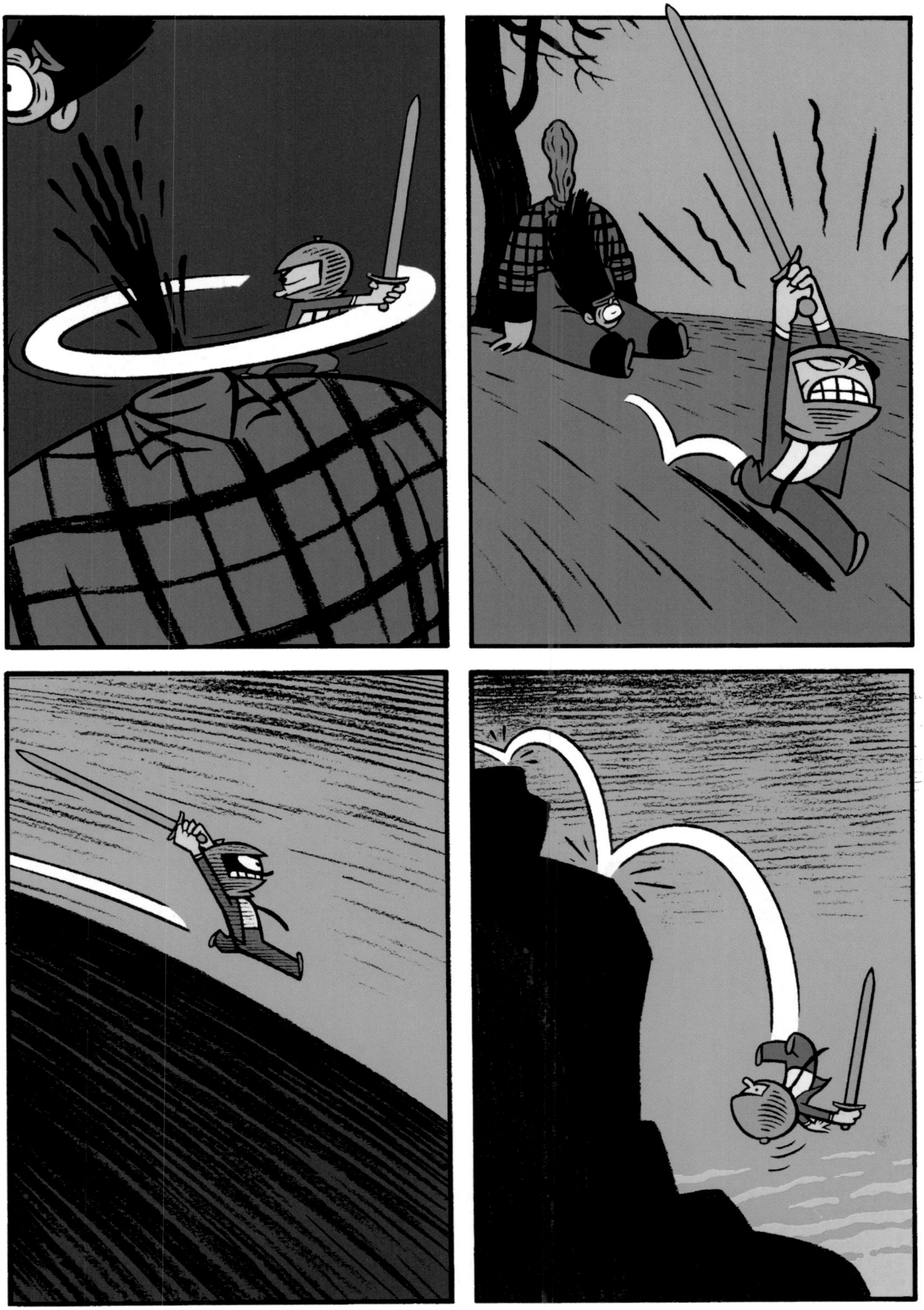

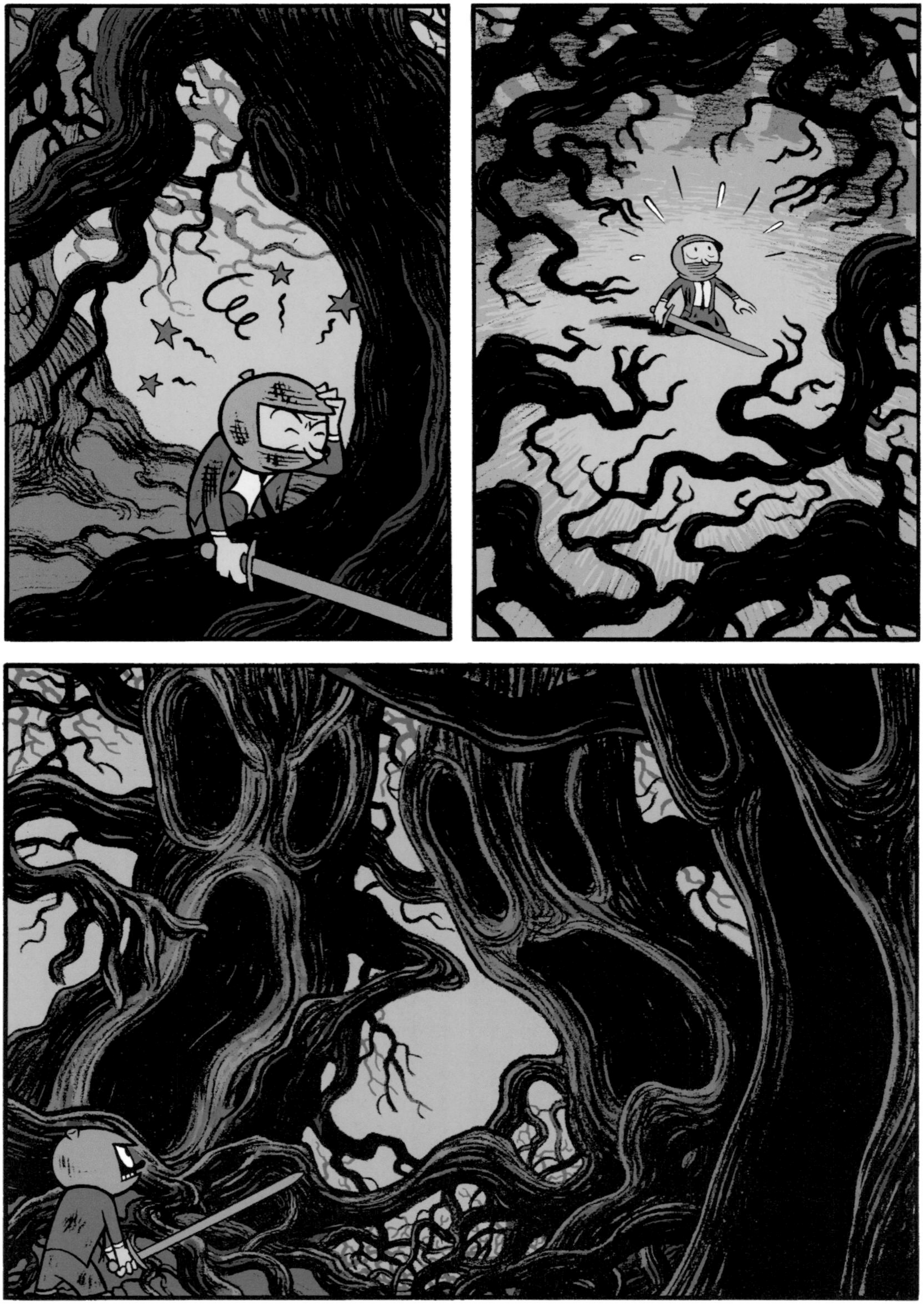

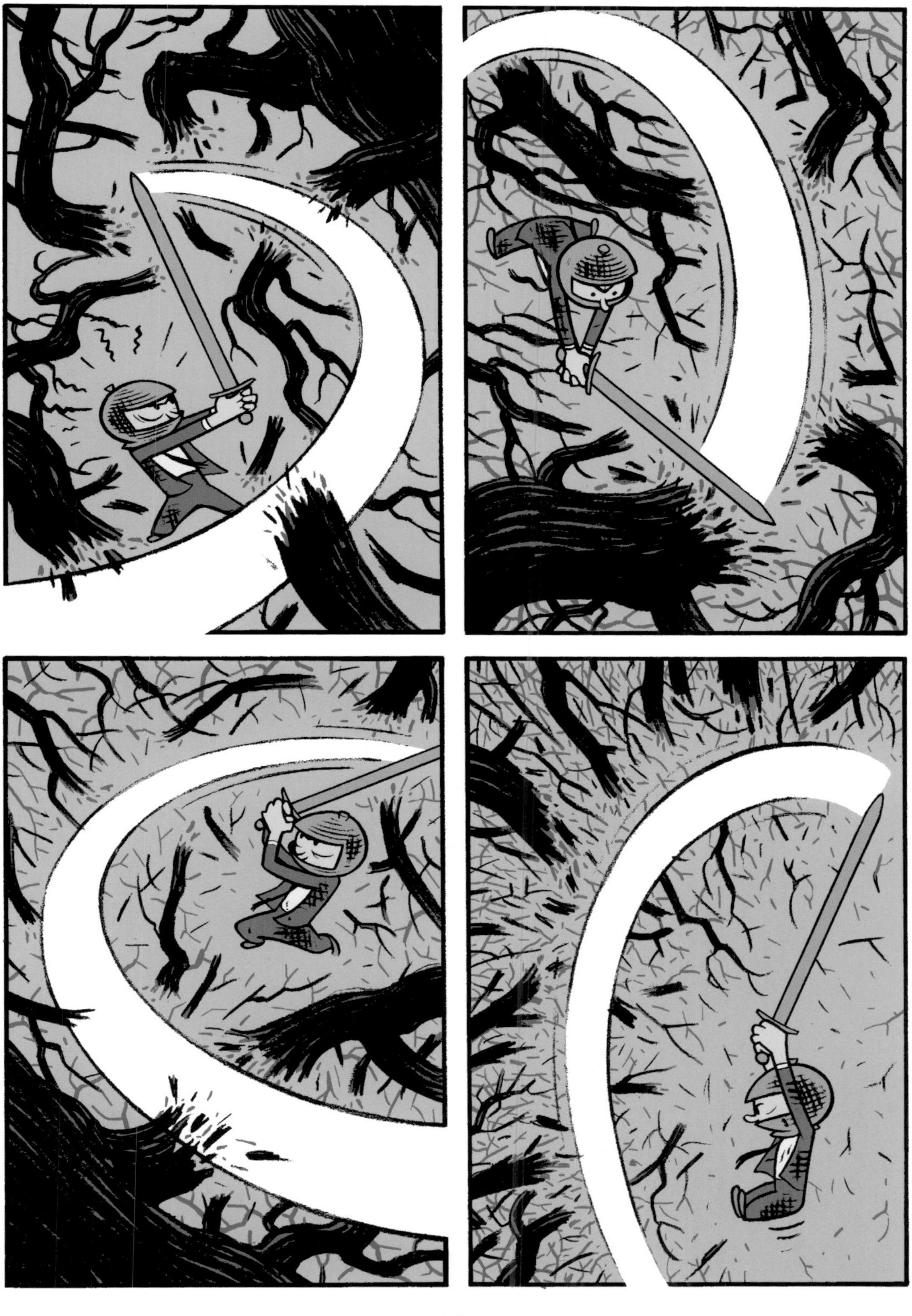

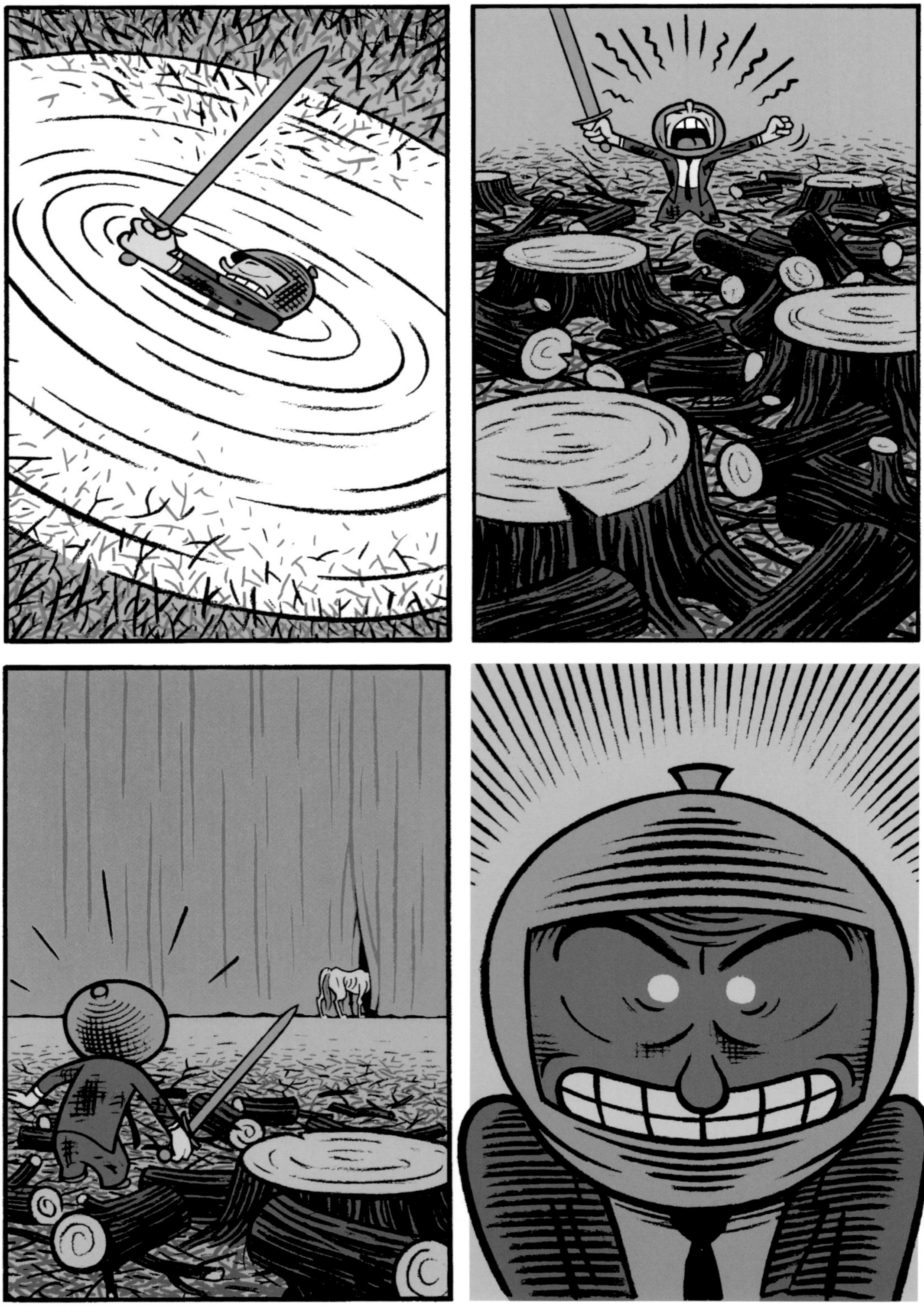

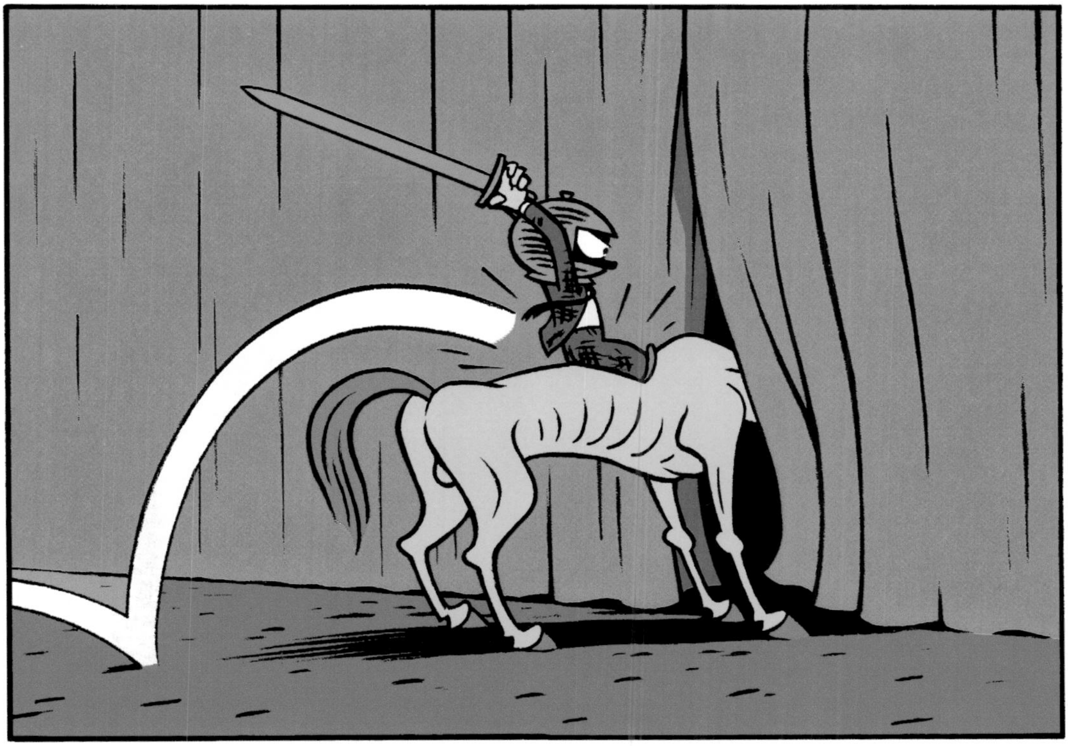

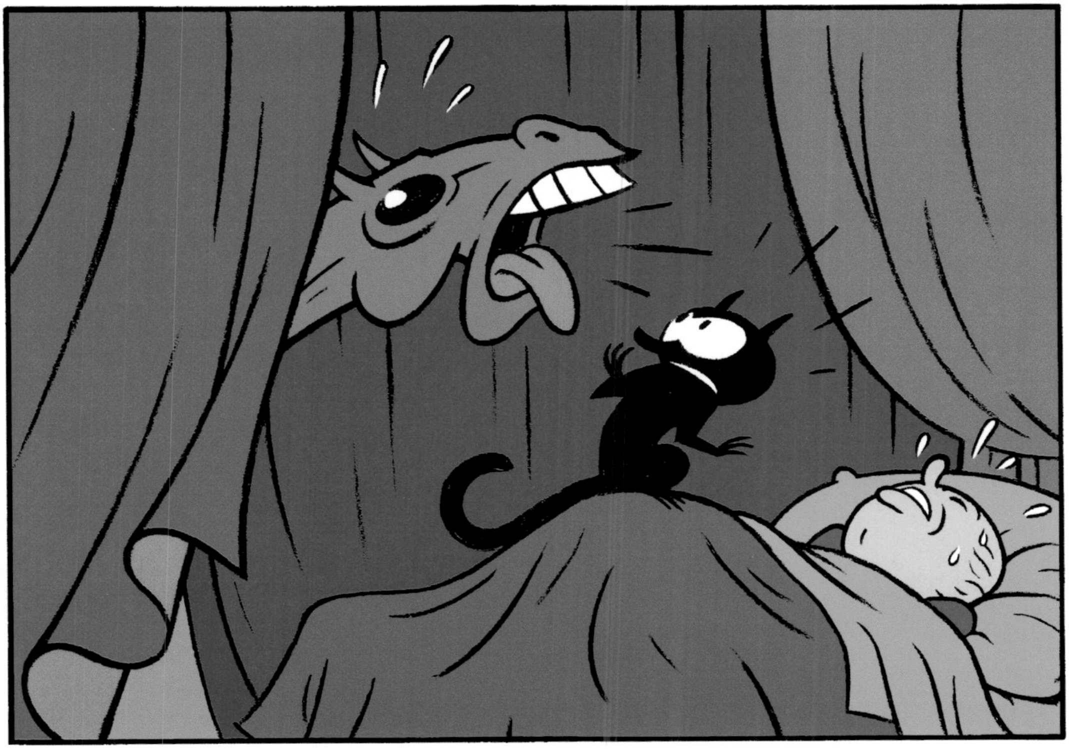

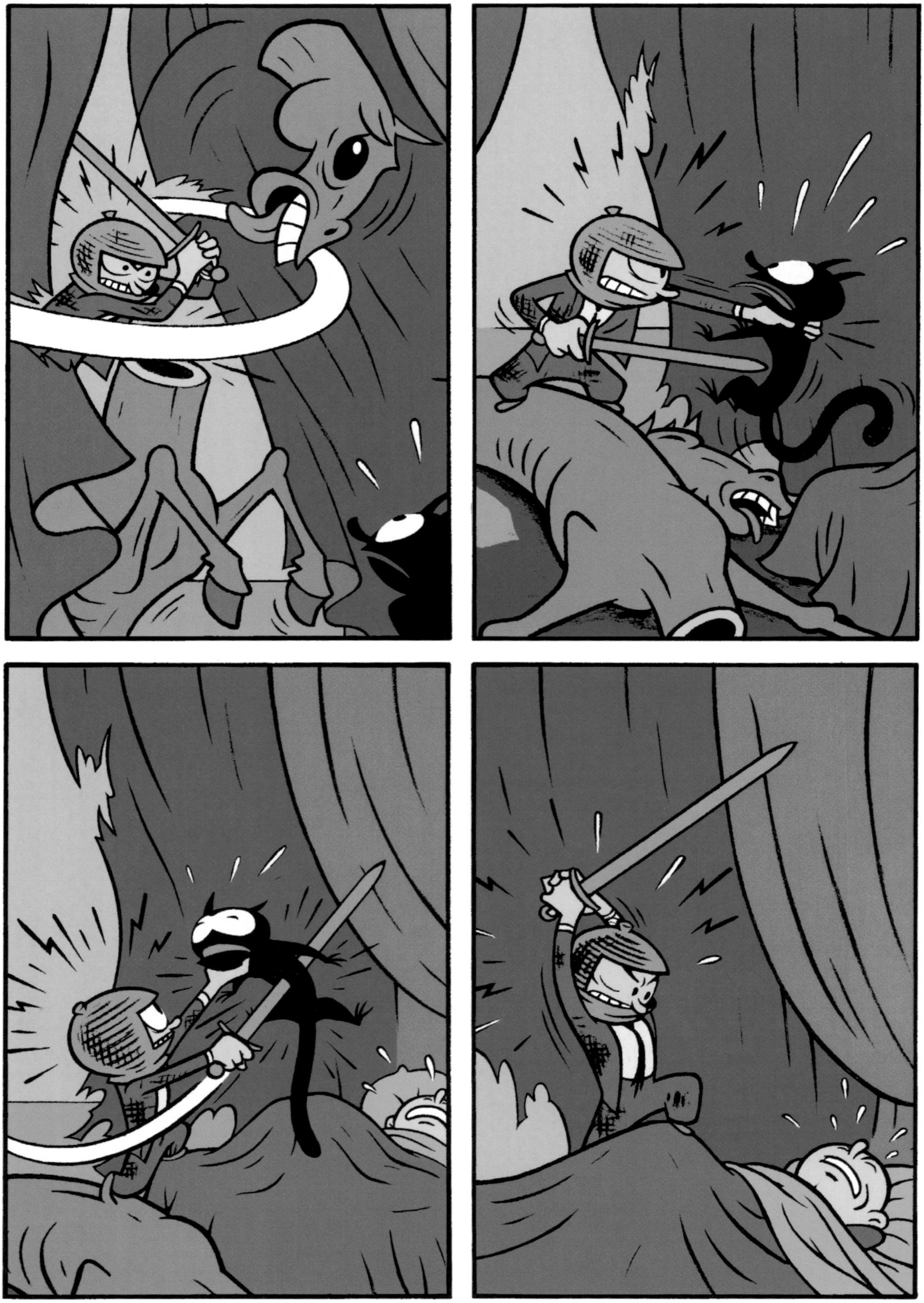

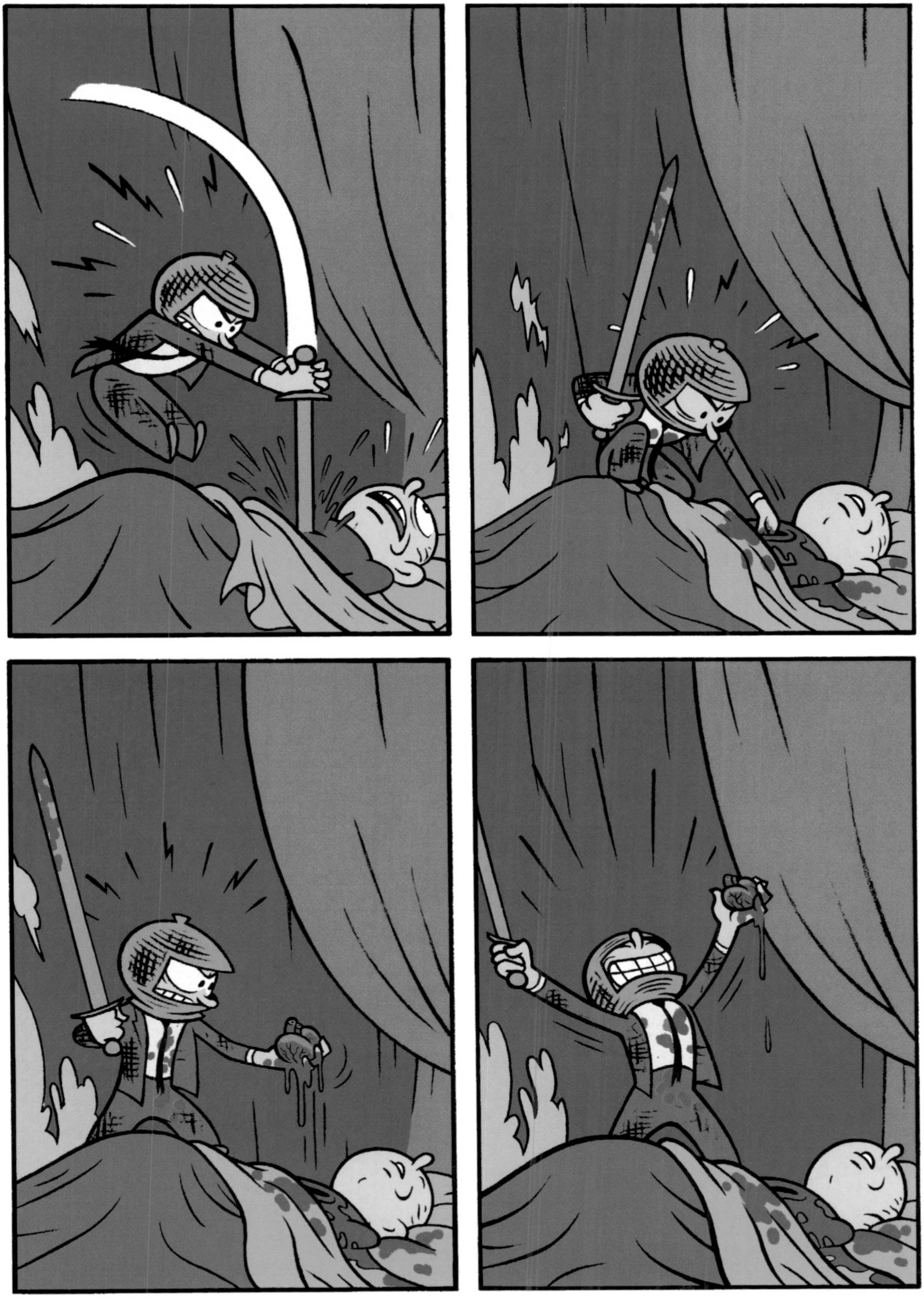

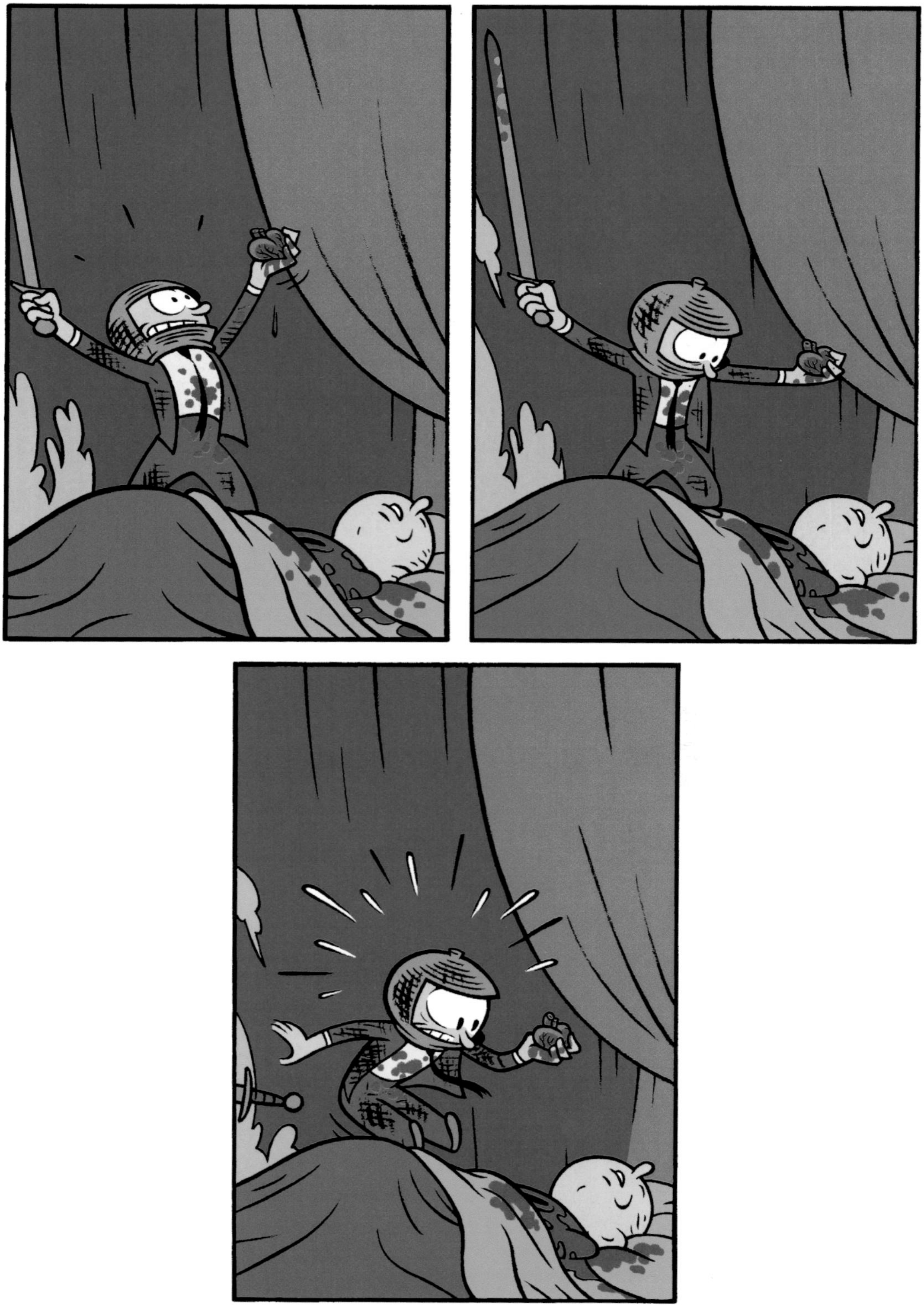

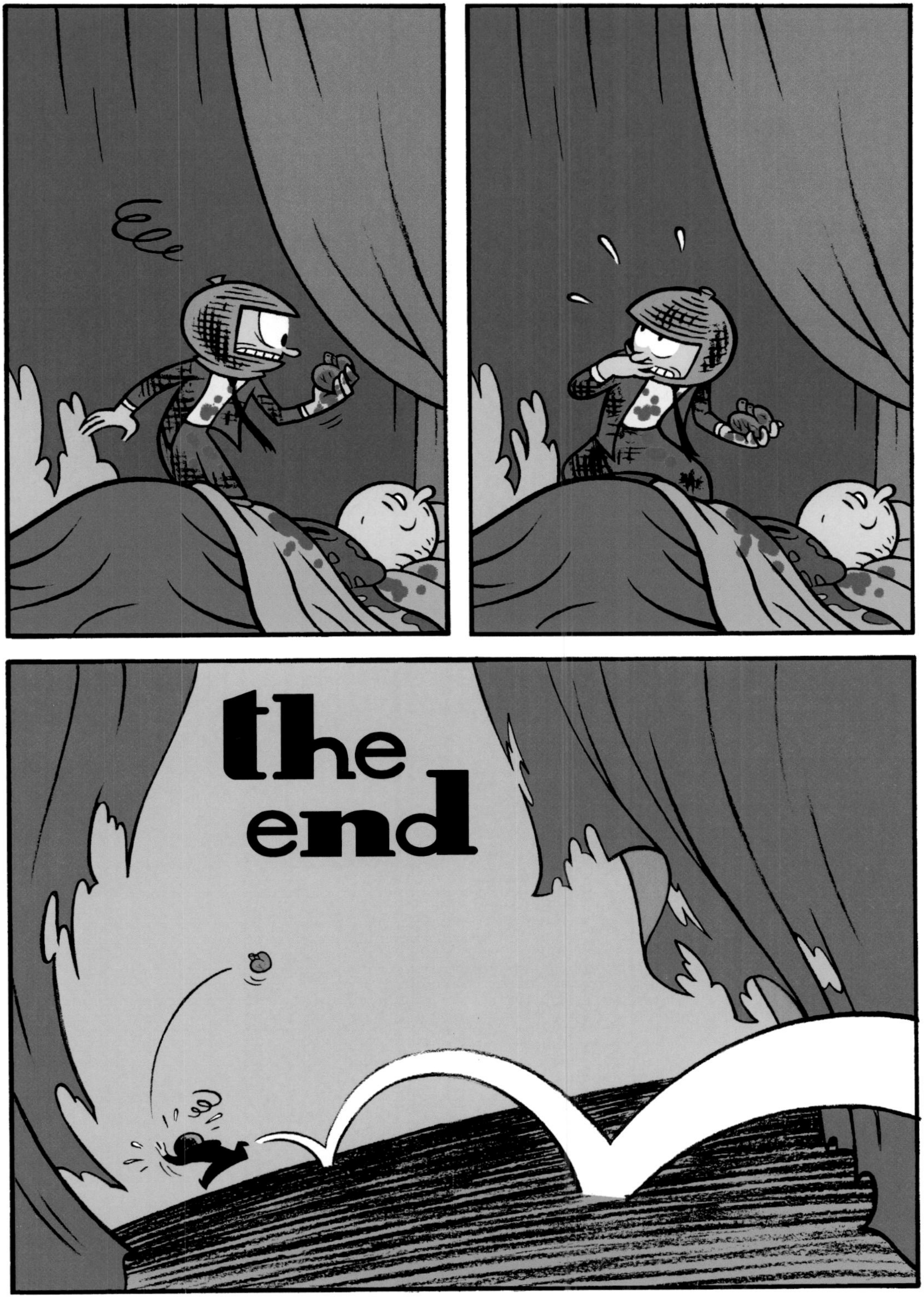
the end

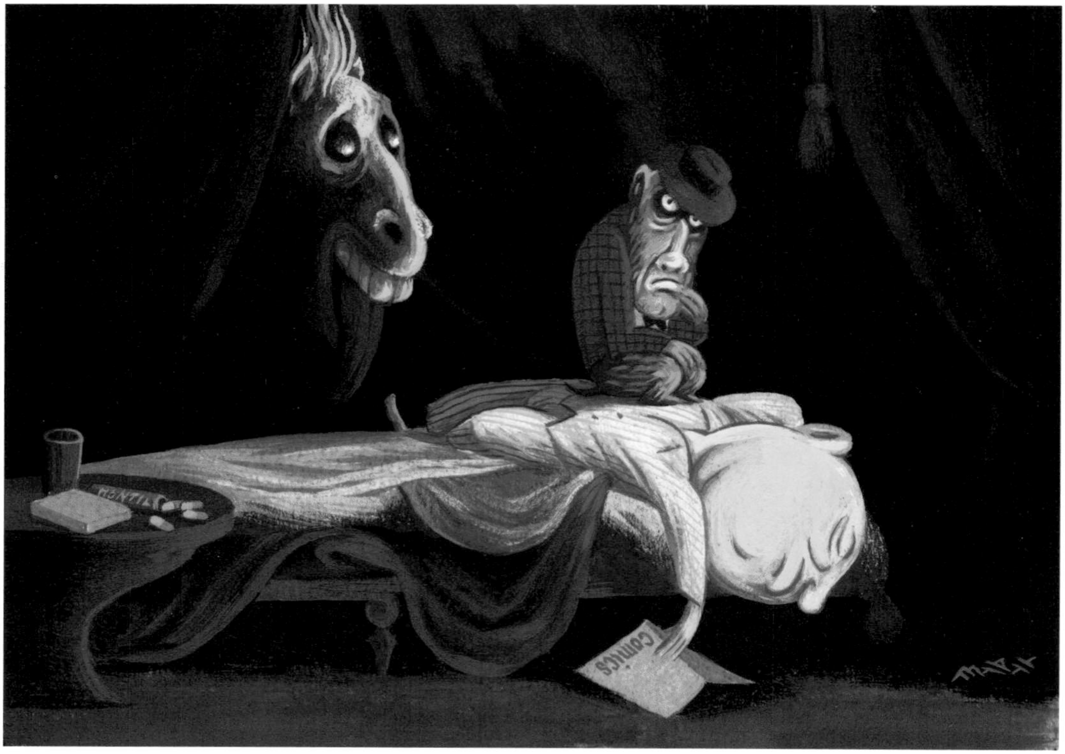
Comics

The Nightmare. Reinterpretation of the painting by Heinrich Füssli (1781).

This book was printed using
high-definition stochastic screening
in Barcelona, Spain, in May of 2006.

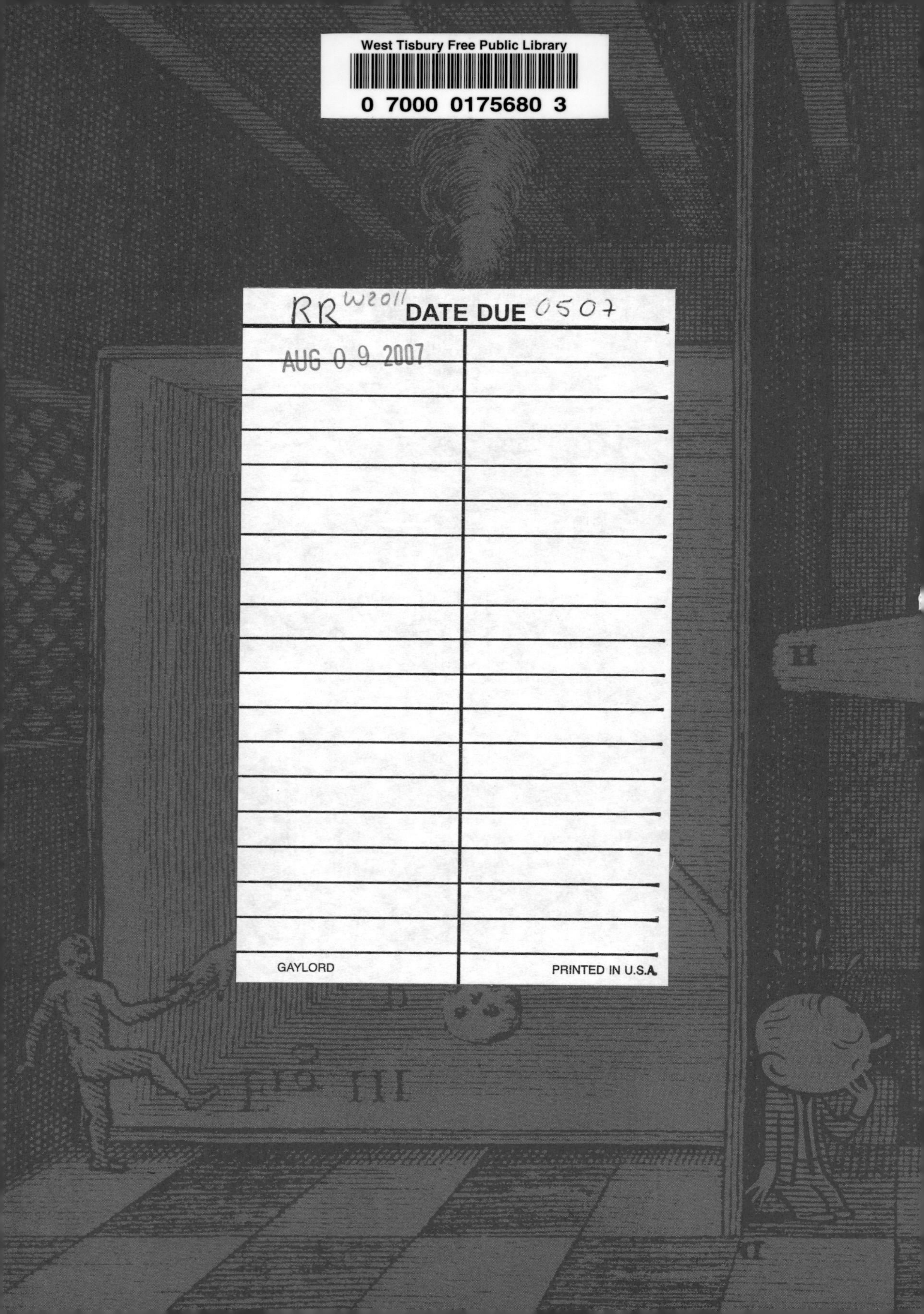